Probably Magic

A Letter for Rosa

JO JEWELL

Published by Pen It! Publications, LLC
812-371-4128   www.penitpublications.com

ISBN: 978-1-952011-82-5

Cover by Donna Cook

Edited by Wanda Williams

Acknowledgments

I am so fortunate to have people in my life that support my writing efforts, cheer me on when I'm feeling inadequate and talk me off the ledge when I'm a nervous wreck.

When I was thirteen years old, I met a girl at school. Our lockers were side by side and who would have thought a lifetime friendship could be formed over combinations that didn't work, new school adjustments, and puberty? But, here we are.

I am dedicating this book to Ruth Lewallen. She's been such a vital part of my life for all my life, that I honestly don't know what I would do without her. We've followed each other through marriages, divorces, childbirth, death, patterns in the tapestry of our lives.

Thank you, Ruth. You're the best bestie a girl could hope for and I hope you know how very much I love and appreciate you.

Thank you, also, for sharing your love of all things paranormal. Though some things we can poke fun at, there are still other things that cannot be explained in the still unexplained world of "the other side."

This was a fun project and I hope it helps you smile.

Dedication

For

Ruth

Chapter One

The year is 2011

At some point in our lives, we decide if we really love our parents or merely tolerate them. At the age of twenty-six, I'm still struggling with that dilemma. Oh, don't get me wrong, they're loving, caring parents and I think the world of them, but I pay the price for their easy-going, humorous, albeit, quirky ways.

Mom ended up pregnant late in life. That's not much of a story. The fact that Dad had a vasectomy some years before that, now, that's a story! When he gasped, "How'd that happen?" Mom shrugged her shoulders and said, "Probably magic." Or so the story goes.

Oh, I guess I should introduce myself since I'm telling you my life story. I am Probably Magic Sarangoski, and I'm pleased to meet you. I've spent my life trying to outrun my name and it has taken me on adventures that, upon reflection, I may have never had if I had been named *Susan*, for example. As if the name wasn't enough of a burden, I have red frizzy hair that follows me like an angry cloud. I don't have cute little freckles scattered daintily across my nose, I have big dark, freckles that look like splotches and I'm stick-thin, all arms and legs, even to this day. I thought I would share some of those adventures with you and to serve as a warning to parents-be kind when you name your children.

My parents were named June and Ward Sarangoski, I kid you not. They were born in the '60s and somehow managed to stop time. They continued to live in the 60's time freeze well up into their years and at the time I left for college, they were still safely ensconced in their happy little bubble. Like the old vinyl records, they insisted on playing on an old stereo the size of a small house, the needle often getting stuck on a track. So was their life, the same 70's songs over and over, stuck on the same track. Mom with her halter tops, beads and long skirts and dad with his bell-bottom pants and round John Lennon glasses. Nothing ruffled them.

When I survived long enough to attend middle school, I was suspicious there was some wacky- tobacky involved, but who was I to judge? They weren't hurting anyone. They still believed in peace, love, and freedom for all. Looking through their rose-colored glasses, they loved me unconditionally.

Meanwhile, on my side of the lifeline, I was bullied unrelentingly. In grade school, the kids were particularly cruel. I was the only kid who got sent to the principal's office on the first day of school for being a smart ass. They all thought my name was a joke. To this day I wonder if maybe it was. Well, it wasn't a very funny joke. Finally, as my story snaked its way through the school administration, I was no longer sent to the school Alcatraz because of my name.

When I complained to my parents about the mean-spirited teasing, my mother would say, "Probably, what would happen if you showered them with kindness? We can bake some cookies for you to take to school! Everyone loves cookies!" I knew better than to eat my mother's cookies, sometimes they tasted funny. My dad would listen with that

3

fatherly nod of his head and get his guitar, "I think there's a song in there somewhere. I should write a song about that", he would say with a snap of his fingers. I guess back in the '70s, funny tasting cookies and music cured just about anything.

In addition to the snickering and name play, I was a tomboy that put all tomboys to shame. I wasn't a girly-girl. In fact, I wore a dress exactly one time and never again after that. I was running away from a group of boys who wanted to poke me with a stick, and I fell. I did a face plant in the gravel, skidding on the heels of my hands while the heels of my feet went flying over my head. My little white cotton panties, with the adorable pink hearts, were fully displayed. The boys were horse laughing and started pointing and chanting, "Look! Magic panties!" Girlhood was officially over.

I learned to fight. I had plenty of practice, so I became quite good at defending myself. Now I went to the principal's office on a regular basis. Now I went to the office for a whole different reason. The principal would call my mother and report I was in trouble again for fighting, while various boys and girls were holding tissues to bleeding noses or holding their arms from me twisting it behind their back. After being mean to me and causing me to fight, I snickered to see them cry. They weren't so tough after all!

And so it went. Mom baked a lot of cookies and dad wrote a bunch of songs, before I finally walked across the stage to receive my high-school diploma. It's humid in June and my hair was screaming in such protest I could not wear the mortarboard with the others. I heard a collective sigh as students and teachers alike no longer had to deal with me. I think the applause and standing ovation was a bit much, but extreme relief can do that.

Now it was time to terrorize my college of choice. And that's when all hell broke loose.

I decided to attend Colorado University in Boulder. It's a small campus surrounded by gorgeous mountain views, wide-open spaces, and a serenity I needed after graduation and the three months spent with Mom and Dad before packing the car up and heading down the road. My backseat held three suitcases, a lamp without a shade, a set of sheets, and four Tupperware boxes of Mom's "special" cookies. She took me aside and whispered, "If you share those with your little friends, you'll be the most popular girl on campus!"

"I don't want to be popular, Mom," I'd said, but she only smiled and winked at me. My parents are weird.

As I pulled into the parking lot, I saw students already sitting under trees reading, a group of boys playing Frisbee, and a clot of girls checking out the man meat. It was all very idyllic and it shocked me at how young these kids looked and acted.

I found a parking place and throwing my duffel bag over my shoulder and removing two of the suitcases from the backseat, I was prepared to start my college career. The only problem I could see was that I still didn't know what I wanted to be when I grew up. I kind of used the finger-poke method, closing my eyes and poking a piece of paper on my bedroom wall with a list of academics the college offered. When I opened my eyes, I gave a great sigh of relief. *Business Administration.* That was pretty generic until I could find my passion. I wasn't holding my breath on that point. Basically, I just wanted freedom. I wanted to breathe air not contained in my parent's denial of a future.

Being a freshman, I had to stay in a dorm. The room was very small with two beds that seemed smaller than a twin size.

I wasn't too sure about that. I could reach out an arm and touch the other bed. Me, being close to six feet tall, had to get used to rolling over into the wall and feet that hung off the end. My roommate was a perky little pixie named Rachel. She seemed nice enough, but I wished I had a camera when she came into the room with me standing there wondering how in the world, I was going to survive an entire year like this.

She was tiny, which made me feel like a giant. She had soft, shiny blond hair, perfectly cut and framing her face, highlighting her cute little button nose. My hair was positively wild. I had the idea that if I let it grow out some, perhaps the weight of it would pull out some of the frizz. No such luck. It was heavy, got in my eyes constantly, and in desperation, I pulled it back into a ponytail with wisps of frizz sticking out around my face. It honestly looked like a bright red bird's nest.

She stopped dead when she stepped into the room, leaned back to check the room number, then straightened her shoulders and threw a suitcase on one of the beds.

"I'm Rachel," she said sticking out her hand.

"I'm Probably," I said receiving her handshake. Her eyes never left me.

"Probably what?" she asked.

"Oh. Probably Magic," I said hoping to clear up any confusion.

She scrunched up her nose and stared at me. "You're probably magic?"

"Ummm…yeah," I said becoming increasingly uncomfortable under her scrutiny.

"Either you have a high opinion of yourself, or you think you're a witch or something," she said without the enthusiastic air she'd had when she arrived.

I was a little stunned until those memories of grade school came back. I laughed and shook my head. "My *name* is Probably Magic Sarangoski!"

"Your NAME is Probably Magic?" she asked watching to see if I was playing a cruel joke on her.

I reached into my backpack and withdrew my wallet and produced my driver's license.

She read it carefully then looked up at me and smiled, "Your parents must have really hated you."

I laughed and just like that, the tension was broken.

She invited me to go to the cafeteria where she was meeting some friends for a Coke or something. I declined, saying instead, I'd like to get settled in. She said okay and flounced out of the room without unpacking or picking her luggage up from the middle of the floor.

I looked at my shadeless desk lamp and said, "This is going to be a very long year."

Chapter Two

I settled into a routine of classes and studying. There were all kinds of activities going on around me, but I really didn't feel I belonged in any of them. I stayed in my room or if I had a weekend without so much studying, I hiked along the mountain trails. I really liked being outside here. The air was always crisp and smelled of pine trees and clear water. It seemed there was always a breeze coming down from the snowcapped mountains and it was refreshing as it chilled my skin, as I sweat under my sweatshirt.

I did okay in my classes, but I need not worry about writing a speech for valedictorian. I was biding my time. I didn't know what that meant, it was just a feeling I had.

One evening, I was returning to my room after swimming laps in the pool. I liked to go right after the evening meal. No one was at the pool, which meant I had it all to myself. I would go back and forth using long, even strokes. I'd get lost in my own thoughts and lose track of how many laps I'd completed. That was okay though, I'd swim until I was tired, excess energy spent.

I was walking across the front lawn when I heard running footsteps behind me.

"Hey, Red! Wait up!" I heard a male voice call.

I kept walking wondering how that person named Red liked being called that. It sounded pretty casual to me. I kind of half-heartedly looked around and saw no one on the lawn with me.

"Red!" the voice called again.

I looked behind to see a rather chubby guy running up to me.

"Me?" I asked pointing to myself.

"Yeah, you, how many Reds do you know?" he asked sarcastically.

I made a show of really concentrating and replied, "Including me? Let's see… That would be none."

Undeterred, he laughed and huffing, and puffing fell into step beside me.

"I've got to ask you a question," he stumbled a little as he tried to straighten his glasses, breathe through his mouth and catch his breath.

"Okay, I'll play. What's your question and then I get to ask you one," I said hoping to discourage any further conversation.

"You get what they're saying about the business tax?" he asked. "I mean, along with state and federal, you got all these other taxes to go along with it. Like Social Security, use tax, employer tax, excise tax. Geez oh, Pete, every time you turn around, there's some other tax!"

I stopped and looked at him full on. "Do I know you? And how do you get off calling me Red?"

He looked a little hurt and a little embarrassed. "Well, shoot, you got all that red hair, hasn't anyone ever called you Red before? And, yeah, we're in Business Functions together. I'm Wally Jenkins. You know, the guy in the back row? And that's really not an answer to my question."

"I can't say I ever noticed you or anyone else in the back row," I snapped.

"Awwww…don't be cruel, Red. The real reason I chased you down is that I want to be friends," he pleaded.

"No, you don't," I replied.

"Yes, yes, I do!"

"No. You don't, Willy."

"Wally."

"Willy, Wally, whatever. You don't even know me," I said as we walked to the dorm door.

"Okay, okay. Tell you what. You meet me on the patio tomorrow and we'll discuss it over ice cream. Then, you can decide. Sound fair?" he coaxed.

"I'm lactose intolerant," I lied.

"That's okay if you lack toes. Not a deal-breaker for friendship!" he shouted as I opened the door. As the door closed, I heard him yell, "Tomorrow at 2:00! On the patio!"

I ran up the stairs to my room and looked out my window behind a curtain to watch him finally walk away. Weirdo.

Truth be told, he was kind of cute in a nerdy kind of way. He wasn't obese but he was chubby. His face was baby round and he had the most gorgeous blue eyes behind black-framed glasses. His hair was very dark, dark brown? Black? I didn't look close enough to notice the exact hue, but he had these curls that didn't want to behave. I guess I could relate to that.

After I'd watched him walk down the path to the boy's dorm, I turned to look in the mirror. I tried to avoid that at all costs, but I was curious as to what Wally saw that I didn't. To be honest, I was really kind of shocked. I'd grown up somewhere along the line. My hair was still bright red and wild, but the freckles had softened, and my eyes were greener than I remembered. My Aunt Jo had once told me green eyes were very special. Less than 3% of the population had true green eyes. She told me that people with true green eyes were often gifted with "sight". Well, duh, unless you were blind, didn't everyone with eyes have sight?

I continued my inventory. Still tall. Last time I was measured I'd been a whopping, too close for comfort to six feet tall, at five feet eleven inches. Getting jeans long enough was a challenge. Thank God I had no plans or desire to wear those high heeled shoes Rachel sported on a daily basis. My skin was soft and dewy, and I seemed to have a natural blush. Rachel was always ragging on me about using makeup, but I really didn't want one more thing to have to learn to do.

I flopped on the bed and stared at the ceiling. What was I going to do about school? I really wasn't interested and started counting the minutes until class was over…before the class even began. I loved being in the mountains, but to my knowledge, the University of Colorado Boulder didn't offer classes on hiking. I didn't want to go back home, that was for sure. I looked at the open closet, well, we called it a closet, it was really just a niche in the wall with a rod for hanging clothes. I didn't mind too much because most of my clothes resided in drawers and those hard plastic totes. The first-time mom visited, she hung up glittery beads, saying a girl needs her privacy when changing clothes. Yeah, well, whatever. I considered taking them down, but a part of me liked having a little bit of home here in the room.

The door burst open and Rachel and her gal pals came stumbling in, laughing, and shrieking. It was annoying.

"We're ordering pizza!" she announced happily.

"Good for you," I muttered.

"Join us, Probably. It'll be fun!" she begged.

"We're going to play Truth or Dare!" a chubby little number named Buffy, gushed.

"Sorry," I apologized. I picked up underwear and a T-shirt and jeans and threw them in a laundry basket. "Tonight is laundry night. You guys have fun."

I made my getaway and as I shut the door, I heard one of them say, "God, she's weird!"

The laughter followed me down the hallway and all the way down to the basement to the laundry room. I liked it down here. It was dank, dark, and empty. I put my clothes in the washer and realized I'd left the laundry supplies in the room. No way in hell I was going back up there, so I just washed them in plain water.

Was I ready for a boyfriend? Boyfriend? Where did that come from? Who said anything about a boyfriend? What if that Wally guy wanted to be my boyfriend? I shook my head. *Get a grip, Probably. No one said a word about boyfriends or girlfriends or anything of the sort.* Come to think of it, I didn't have any girlfriends either. In fact, I didn't really have any friends. I was a true, dyed in the wool, loner. I could be likable. Right? I practiced smiling in the shiny chrome of the paper towel dispenser. Yep, I looked like some deranged giant. Loneliness grabbed hold of me. I took my sopping clothes and flung them in the dryer. Stupid stuff. Life was full of stupid stuff and here I was stuck right in the thick of it.

I climbed the stairs and snuck out the door. As long as I was back by midnight, the doors would still be open. I walked the deserted paths to the buildings and just enjoyed the sounds of the night, the muted rock and roll coming from a few of the rooms, the lighted windows as students crammed for the next day's lessons. Should I be studying?

I gave it due consideration, then shook my head, Nah. I liked to be surprised by what I did or didn't know. I walked out of the gate and down the road. Only a couple of cars passed me. I just kept walking. I wasn't even sure where the road led, exactly. If memory served me, there was a quaint little town, fed by the college students. The bars, restaurants, and novelty shops were more than happy to gobble up the kid's allowances, or at least what was left from the college bookstores. Mom and Dad made sure I didn't want for anything, which was good and fortunate, but I was like them (I shivered), I didn't need much.

I came upon a noisy hole-in-the-wall student bar called, Bloody Marys. It was dim and loud music made the pavement beneath my feet vibrate. I could hear laughter and glasses and shouts of drunken glee. I stepped inside. As my eyes adjusted, I saw couples dancing, boys flirting, and girls trying to stick out their bosoms as far as possible. I sauntered up to the bar and ordered a Coke. A riot of laughter exploded from a table and as one of the boys leaped from his chair, glasses clinked and fell to the floor, shattering.

I watched with detached amusement.

"Hey, Red!" came a shout from across the room.

I ducked making myself as small as possible, at least five feet ten inches tall, and escaped to a dark corner with minimal activity. A couple sat at a table making kissy faces and I averted my eyes and concentrated on my Coke. I sat there for a few minutes and got bored. I looked around me and saw a dark hallway to the left of me. No restroom signs and come to think of it, I could use one of those signs about now.

I went to stand by the hallway to survey the room to see if I could see the restroom sign. A young man in a leather jacket, white T-shirt, and jeans rolled up at the ankles rushed by me without so much as a 'pardon me' and hurried down the hallway. Tired, cranky, or something, it just hit me wrong. I went after him to give him a lesson in manners. He pushed out a back door and disappeared outside. *Must be the back lot,* I thought to myself. Well, so much the better!

I followed him out the back door and saw a vintage Cadillac convertible with three other boys. Two were sitting on the back of the back seat, waving the rude boy to hurry up, the driver looked straight at me. I marched up to the car ready to give these boys a piece of my mind when the car began to roll away. I didn't hear the engine start or tires on the pavement. I couldn't even hear their laughter. I shook my head and wondered if the obscene noise level in the bar had damaged my hearing. I walked out into the lot and saw the car spin out, gravel flying. A stone struck my cheek and it stung like fire. I reached up and felt it, very sure it was bleeding. I ran after the car but suddenly I skidded to a halt. It had disappeared. Less than a block away, it just vanished into thin air.

Chapter Three

"**W**hat're you doing out here, Red?"

I whirled around and saw Wally standing in the doorway, holding the door open.

I pointed to the place the Caddy had just been and stammered, "Did you…I saw…and then it was…"

"You're not making any sense," he said coming out into the lot to stand by me.

"Some guy…I followed him out here…then …"

Wally looked at me no longer smirking. "You okay, Red?"

As if coming out of a trance, I suddenly heard myself and he was right. I wasn't making any sense. What just happened?

"I need to go back to the dorm now," I said flatly. "I really need to go home."

"I can give you a ride. I'm not sure you should be wandering around alone," he offered. "You sure you're okay?"

I shook my head but said, "Yeah, I'm fine. I just need to go home." I turned and began walking. Wally ran to catch up to me.

"I'll walk with you if you won't let me give you a ride then," he said.

"No. I prefer to be alone," I snapped at him much harsher than I intended.

I left him standing there, watching me as I stumbled on loose gravel. I just needed to get home. Every step I took brought back the scene. I couldn't hear anything and yet they were there, then they were gone. What vintage car made no noise at all? It just didn't make any sense.

Before I knew it, I was at the gate. Great. It was locked. I looked around and saw fencing on either side. I heaved and puffed and panted but finally made it over the fence, dropping down into the dew dampened grass. I ripped my jeans in the process and scraped my knee. It was too dark to see if it was bleeding, which made me think of my cheek. I gingerly rubbed it with my finger and sure enough, there was blood coming from the little puncture the loose gravel had made. It was little, and to be honest, the only way I knew it was blood was because it had dried somewhat and flaked off when I rubbed it.

Limping, I made my way to the dorm. The door was locked. Of course, it was locked! It was dark-thirty and all decent folks were in their beds asleep. The music had died, only a couple of lights were still on. I looked under the hedges and found a couple of pebbles. I tossed them at my room window hoping Rachel would hear. I missed. Crap! I found a couple more and tossed those. One found the target and it wasn't much more than an unsatisfying tap.

Giving up, I sat on the step. All the kids carried cellphones these days. I'd never gotten around to getting one. There was no one to call or to call me, so it just seemed like a waste of money. That was a stupid reason, for now, I was thinking of accidents while hiking, getting stuck at the bus station, running late for class, all kinds of things I could use a cellphone for that didn't require much social interaction.

I leaned my head against the brick balustrade and thought about that stupid car again. I didn't understand what happened and then felt much better when I'd finally convinced myself it was my mind playing tricks on me. I was so mad and so hell-bent on picking a fight, I wasn't paying attention to any noise they were making. I'd lost sight of the car when it turned at the next block. This is why it is not a good idea to leave me unsupervised. My mind was warped, and my imagination carried me away. I sighed, pulled my hoodie tighter around me, and closed my eyes.

"Oh my God, Probably!" a screech that quickly brought me awake. I had fallen asleep on the step and my neck had the mother of all kinks in it. Rachel stood over me, clutching her books.

"What time is it?" I mumbled.

"Better question, what're you doing out here?" Rachel demanded.

"I guess I fell asleep," I said stating the obvious.

"You're going to be late to class! And what did you do to your knee? It's bleeding!" she continued to shout. Did I give her the impression I was hard of hearing?

I looked down at my ripped jeans and the blood-soaked fringes of the hole dumbly. I put a finger to my cheek and there was nothing there.

I looked up at Rachel and said with all the sincerity I could muster, "I kinda had it out with a mountain lion last night."

"A mountain lion?" she said disbelieving my reasoning. "You're so weird. No wonder no one likes you," she shot back.

"Wally likes me," I said in my defense.

"Who's Wally, the mountain lion?" she spat and flounced away.

18

I limped up the stairs and went into the bathroom to clean up. I put a band-aid on the cut, changed clothes and inspected my face in the mirror. There was no mark whatsoever on my cheek. I sighed and thought that must have been part of the dream.

I was making my way painfully to my second class, having totally missed the first. Mrs. Carmen, my business tax professor met me in the hallway.

"I'm to tell you if you ever showed up that Dean Ragsdale wants to see you," she said with a dismissive air.

"The Dean? What for?" I asked though I had a pretty good idea.

She gave me an exasperated sigh and went into the room, leaving me to stand there until I was so motivated to go to the Dean's office. This brought back painful memories too. Being hauled to the principal's office in grade school, middle school, and high school. I considered making a stop at my dorm room and taking Dean Ragsdale some of mom's 'special' cookies. I thought better of it and just walked as slow as possible to his office.

"What happened last night, Miss Sarangoski?" the Dean said giving me the evil eye.

"What do you mean?" I stalled.

"Miss Sarangoski, we have a curfew in place for a reason. We expect all our students to be in their dorm rooms getting the rest they need for a full educational experience. There's a reason we don't allow our students to run all willy-nilly, getting into trouble. Or, what if you were in an accident? We'd be thinking Miss Sarangoski was tucked away in her bed fast asleep. How could we get help to you?

I understand that the college experience, especially for freshmen, is most likely the first time most have been away from home, without a parent's eyes watching every move they make, but there are still rules to follow."

I was watching his mouth move up and down but all I heard was *yada-yado-blah blah, Miss Sarangoski. Yibbety, jabbery, blah*. I zeroed in on a long, stray hair in his mustache. It was thick like fishing line and white as snow. Upon closer inspection, I realized it was a nose hair! Oh my gosh! A giggle escaped me, and I tried to cover it with a discreet cough. He had *huge* pores!

"You find being expelled funny, Miss Sarangoski?" he blubbered.

"No, sir," I replied becoming suddenly alert. "I deeply appreciate the opportunity to get my education at such a fine institution. I know you're all working hard to."

Horrified, the laughter bubbled up and spewed forth like the Old Faithful Geyser. I couldn't stop! The more I tried to contain it, the more it wanted release.

Dean Ragsdale was not amused.

Through the hysterical laughter, I noticed his face turning beet red, the vein in his forehead throbbing, and his jowls positively vibrating with anger. I thought he was going to have a stroke! I laughed so hard, no sound was coming out and suddenly, I snorted and had to pee with an urgency I'd never felt before.

He finally stood, walked to the door, and opened it, "Your expulsion papers will be ready by the end of this week."

That finally sobered me, and I realized he was actually talking about kicking me out of school! That meant I would be sent back home! Okay, that's not funny at all.

"I'm so sorry, Dean Ragsdale, I truly am! I don't know, I think I've been under too much stress lately. Really, this isn't how I am. Please, don't kick me out. Everyone deserves a chance to make it right, right?" I begged him.

He stood uncertainly still holding the door open.

"I promise, it will never happen again. I was just…so…tense, I went for a walk and lost track of time. I feel better when I'm outside, it calms me," I spoke very fast, making it up as I went along.

"I promise," I said beseechingly.

"Well, okay, but this will go as a black mark on your record and mind you, little missy, I'll be watching you like a hawk," he relented. "Never again. No more trouble out of you. You hear?"

I nodded vigorously and stood, extending my hand. "Thank you, Dean. I promise no more trouble. I screwed up and what I did was wrong. Please accept my apology."

He didn't extend his hand in solidarity and only nodded his head to the open door.

I walked out of his office and went back to my room. I needed peace and quiet for just a little while. That was a close call. I didn't want to go back home, that was for sure. I didn't belong here, that was for sure as well. Stuck between two rocks is never a good position. I needed to clear my head. My classes were almost over for today anyway. Tuesdays were my short days. This gave me valuable study time. Instead, though, I picked up my backpack and headed to my car. This time I took my car. I'd had enough walking for a while. I'd had enough of professors, of math, of being forced to interact, of unexplained dreams. I'd just plain had enough.

Chapter Four

When I got to the car, I yanked open the door and threw my backpack onto the passenger seat. I got behind the steering wheel and just sat there. Dang, it! I got back out of the car and walked across the front lawn and into the courtyard. I saw Wally sitting at a table with his laptop open. I plopped down in the second chair and glared at him.

His eyebrows shot up as he looked at me in surprise. "You came!"

"Yeah, so what did you want to discuss that was so important you had trouble leaving my doorstep?" I groused. "Yeah, I saw you standing there like some lost puppy."

Wally smiled, "So you were watching me? That's progress!"

"What do you want from me, Wally? I don't have a damned thing to give you," I said suddenly tired of the game.

"I want to know what last **night** was all about," he said turning serious.

"I believe you said there was ice cream involved," I reminded him.

"I did!" he exclaimed and jumped up to fetch ice cream. He came back moments later with two containers containing two scoops of vanilla ice cream, hot fudge, nuts, sprinkles, cherries, whipped cream, and fresh strawberries. They looked like an ice cream parlor exploded.

He shrugged and explained, "I didn't really know what you liked so I got all the most popular things I figured angry, red-haired girls like."

I couldn't help it, I smiled. I didn't want to smile because that would only encourage this inane behavior, but it slipped out before I could stop it.

"So, you know a lot of red-haired girls, do you?"

He blushed and smiled, "I've met my share, but never one like you."

"Wally, first off, I think you're crazy to keep after someone like me. I'm a loner. I answer to no one but myself. I'm not a girly girl, I'm not interested in dating *anyone*, and I sure as hell don't know a thing about sex. So, don't get any ideas," I said pointedly.

Wally thoughtfully put a spoonful of ice cream in his mouth and crunched a nut. When he swallowed, he thought a few more seconds. "Well, that certainly lays out the ground rules. Okay, first off, I've been told I'm crazy enough that it doesn't even phase me now. Secondly, I can tell you're a loner wannabe, but I don't believe it. I think you've always been alone and so you think that's how it's supposed to be. Thirdly, who said I was going to ask you out on a date?"

"You weren't?" I asked embarrassed by my hasty assumption.

"Oh, yeah! Damned straight I was! I have duly been warned off, though, so is just hanging out acceptable?"

"I'm mean to you. Why would you want to date me?" I surprised myself by asking. I sounded pathetic like I was fishing for compliments or something. A movement caught my eye and my vision was drawn to it. It was a guy standing by, almost behind, the fountain. He was staring at us. No. He was staring at me.

Wally noticed my gaze had shifted and cast a glance over his shoulder. He continued with his tirade. "I'm just going to pretend you did not just ask me that, you wouldn't like the answer anyway. Where was I? Oh, yeah, sex. Sex is great. I can teach you," he said with a wink. He looked over his shoulder again, "What are you staring at?"

"That guy over there is staring at me. I'm starting to feel uncomfortable."

Wally looked at the fountain, "What guy?"

"That guy!" I exclaimed in frustration. "There's only one guy over there, what do you mean, 'what guy'?"

Wally pushed his chair back and sauntered over to the fountain. He walked the full circle around it and then put both arms out to show me there was no guy standing by the fountain.

"I have to go," I said abruptly and left my melting, untouched ice cream to take its chances with either the Colorado sun or Wally.

I was shaking when I got to my car. I couldn't get the key in the ignition and my frustration was getting the better of me. Was I going crazy? Was I going to end up like Aunt Jo? People whispered about her and I remember there was some talk about maybe sending her to a place for people who lost their minds. Was it hereditary? By the way, whatever happened to Aunt Jo?

The memory of last night slammed into my brain. I wasn't sure I was in any condition to drive, but I had to escape. I had to get my mind off being crazy. I was young! Young people don't go crazy all at once, do they?

I drove much too fast and made it into the little town in a fraction of the time it took me to walk it. I drove around taking in all the little shops and busy sidewalks. With some relief, I knew none of these people knew me. They wouldn't know if I was crazy or not. I'll try to act normal. I practiced my smile in the rearview mirror. Nope, I still looked like a deranged serial killer. Maybe I could look pensive, I was a student after all.

I parked the car and walked on the sidewalk. I peered into shop windows but didn't see anything of interest to me. Trendy clothes, sparkly shoes, computers, knick-knacks to remember our college experience, it was all just stuff. My stomach rumbled and I remembered I hadn't eaten since yesterday afternoon. I stopped at a sidewalk vendor and got two hotdogs, one with chili sauce and onions, the other with sauerkraut and bacon bits. I munched on the hotdogs while sitting on the ledge of a planter. I was still hungry. I meandered to a small burger joint and ordered onion rings and a Coke. I got extra Southwest sauce and mechanically dipped an onion ring, and munched, slurp Coke, dip onion ring, slurp, dip, slurp.

When I'd finished eating, I continued down the sidewalk. At the very end was a house painted yellow with white trim. An arched trellis was full of peach roses and a yard full of wildflowers. It was cool and shady under the Maple trees and a giant oak spread its massive branches over the yard. It was all contained within a white picket fence which completely enclosed the lot. A white gate was suspended inside the arch.

A brass sign nailed onto the gate read: *Whispers Bookstore*

Curious, I lifted the latch and went inside the yard. It sure looked like a house, was I supposed to knock? It said it was a bookstore though, so it was public domain, right? What if it was both? Someone opened a bookstore in their *home*. I really was in a quandary of what to do when the door opened, and a grandmotherly woman came out with a watering can.

"OH!" she exclaimed, "I didn't realize anyone was here! Come in, come in!"

"If this is a bad time…" I began.

"Oh, heavens no, dear. Please, do come in. I just took some chocolate chip cookies out of the oven. Come in, have some warm cookies, and look at the books. You're sure to find exactly what you're looking for," she invited me in.

The inside did smell heavenly! Even with the hot dogs and onion rings still laying like a rock in my stomach, my mouth began to water. To distract myself, I began looking at her book collection. It was impressive, indeed. Old collections from William Wordsworth, Elizabeth Browning, a full collection of Shakespeare! I began to feel a peace I hadn't felt in a long while.

"Here, dear, sit on the divan and read and munch on cookies. Would you like a glass of milk or a cup of tea?" she beamed.

I wondered if she didn't have many customers and was lonely down here at the end of a dead-end street. I didn't see any textbooks at all, just great works of literary art. I felt myself being propelled to the divan. She still had her gardening gloves on.

"Milk sounds lovely," I said. She rushed off for the milk and cookies. I noticed a book laying on the coffee table and turned my head sideways to read the title. *Finding Your Inner Peace.* I picked it up and read the insert. It was about using meditation to ease the stress within and to find a happy medium in the chaotic day-to-day.

The woman came back with the refreshments and set them on the table.

"Oh! I see you picked one about meditation," she smiled.

"No, it was…" I began.

"I'll tell you a secret. I never realized just how much pressure and stress I had in my everyday life until I learned meditation," she said with a knowing nod of her head.

"I'm really not the meditating type," I dismissed her.

"Sweetie, we're humans, we're all meditating types. It's human nature to seek peace. We are constantly roaming around, trying the new next best thing, and then we wonder why we lose interest, feel lost. It's because we seek outside distractions instead of inside calm. Do you know what your biggest enemy is?" she asked looking over her gold-rimmed glasses.

I dumbly shook my head.

"Fear!" she exclaimed. "Fear destroys happiness, it destroys moments meant to be cherished, it destroys a drive to succeed."

I watched her become more animated as she continued her rant. Sure, she looked like what I always pictured Mother Goose to look like in human form. A soft, cloud of snow-white hair, short and round, naturally rosy cheeks, and those adorable glasses sitting at the end of her nose. She droned on about meditation being the sword to vanquish fear and I wondered how many customers were chained in her dark, dank basement who she only fed on Tuesdays and Thursdays until they could take that sword and slay the evil dragon called Fear.

I rose abruptly from the divan, already feeling the chains around my wrists. I needed to escape! She looked at me in surprise.

"I just remembered, I, uh, have a student hall meeting in about thirty minutes." I backed toward the door. Oh, that old dragon called Fear was rearing his royal head inside me right now. "Thank you so much for the cookies and milk…"

"Vera," she said through a smile. "Just call me Vera and I do hope you'll come again. You're quite an interesting young lady. I enjoyed our visit very much," she said sweetly.

"Um, of course. I enjoyed meeting you too, Vera," I said as I got closer to the door.

She came toward me and my stomach fell right to the floor and my heart hammered in my chest. She stopped in front of me and handed me the book. "You forgot your book, dear." She smiled up at me with the innocence of a child.

"I don't have any money on me right now," I hedged.

"Oh, pooh! Don't worry about that! The next time you're in town, drop by. If you like it, we'll settle then. If you don't like it, then you haven't spent your hard-earned money," she offered.

She opened the door and stepped out on the porch with me hot on her heels. She turned and looked at the mountains. With a great sigh, she said softly, "That's where I slay my dragons."

I opened my mouth, but no words came out. She smiled at me and went back into the house shutting the door behind her.

What just happened? I asked myself. I made sure she wasn't watching me through the window, and I picked a peach rose from the arch. I wanted to make sure it was real and not like the boys in the Cadillac or the guy by the fountain. A thorn tore through my thumb and blood bubbled up. *Yeah, okay, but will it still be bleeding when I get back to my room?*

Chapter Five

The sun was making its way behind the mountain range and long shadows were cast across the campus. I pulled into my parking space and looked at my thumb. Still bleeding. That's good. I held the book for a moment just staring at it. Fear. Vera said fear was our greatest enemy. A thought popped into my head. Had I always lived in Fear? Fear of not belonging, fear of getting stuck like my parents. Fear of rejection and ridicule because of my name? Had I been so afraid of not fitting in that I actually did everything in my power to NOT fit in? It was a sobering thought. I was so lost in thought as I made my way to my dorm that I didn't see Wally lurking behind a tree.

"Hey, Red!" he shouted. I wish he'd stop calling me that! I kept walking and, as usual, he had to run to catch up with me.

"What?" I said taking even longer strides.

"What happened this afternoon? You were kind of freaked out and left in such a hurry. I have to admit you are one jumpy woman. We don't have to have sex until you're ready. I promise," he said earnestly.

I stopped short causing him to bump into the back of me.

"What in the name of all that's holy, are you talking about?" I glared at him.

He looked a little baffled. "Well, we were talking about sex and then you said you saw…anyway, it was weird all the way around."

"Welcome to my world," I snarked at him.

"Oh! That's what I like most about you!" he hurried to clarify.

"Wally, I suppose some people find your persistence endearing, but I'm really not in the mood. I've had a…" I stopped midsentence. I was going to say *weird day*, but was that validating what he just stated?

"Red, sometimes you scare me. You're a jumpy giant of a woman and sometimes, I just have to wonder what's rattling around in that interesting brain of yours," he tried smiling.

"You know what, Wally? Me too," I confessed, "Me too."

Wally looked at the ground and scuffed at an imaginary rock and said, "Red, I know we don't really know each other really well yet, but I want you to know, I'm your friend, or at least I want to be your friend. You can talk to me," he held his hand up to stop any comment from me. "I do think you're weird, but that's just it. All these other girls are running around trying to impress the guys and trying to act much sexier than is age-appropriate, but you are genuine. You don't put on any airs. What you see is what you get, with you. I like that. I don't like playing cutesy games and then finding out it was all an illusion. I know what I'd be getting with you and I like what I've seen so far."

I could do no more than just stare at him. It was such a heartfelt speech; I didn't even feel like sniping at him. He looked up at me and for the first time, I really noticed he had ocean blue eyes. I felt my shoulders slump in defeat.

"You make me sound like a…a…real human, Wally. I don't, can't, see what you see in me. My head is always in chaos, I'm forever trying to figure out what's going on. Sometimes I feel like I'm going crazy," I admitted to him.

"Well, don't go getting the idea I think you're perfect or nothin' because your ears are way too big for your head. What size shoe do you wear? Size 26?" he said with all the seriousness of a heart attack. I noticed he hadn't mentioned my wild hair or my height, both attributes that made me extremely self-conscious.

I burst out laughing and clapped him on the shoulder, "I guess I could use a friend."

There was a bit of an awkward silence as we both stood there trying not to look at each other. Finally, I held up my book and said, "Well, I guess I'd better get going. I've got a book to read."

The relief on his face was evident and he nodded his head, "Yeah, me too. I need to do some studying for exams tomorrow."

At that moment a snowflake fell and landed in his black hair. I looked up and realized the sun was long gone and evening clouds were crowding the sky. Some were a muted shade of gray. More snowflakes began to drift down from the sky. Without a proper goodbye, we both turned and walked to our dorms.

I ran up the stairs to my room and skidded to a halt when I came through the door. Rachel's bed was bare, the closet empty, and the dump truck full of beauty supplies had been cleared out of the bathroom. I stood in the center of the room dumbstruck. One of the girls, who lived down the hall, passed the door and I called out to her. I could tell she didn't want to get into a conversation with me, but she was polite, and she did come back.

"Where's Rachel? Did she quit?" I asked.

"She transferred to a room on the first floor," she said simply.

"Why?" I asked and I immediately didn't know why I asked. It wasn't like there was a blooming friendship there.

"I don't know," the girl said avoiding my eyes.

"Yeah, you do. You guys are always talking back and forth. I know she said something," I pushed on, still not knowing why I was so insistent. I was a glutton for punishment, that's why.

"Well, um, you see, it's like…well, Probably, even you have to admit you're a bit of an odd duck."

"But that's no reason to move lock, stock, and barrel without so much as a word!"

"Probably, she was afraid of you, okay? You happy now?" the girl blurted out and then fled down the hall to the shower.

Afraid of me? What the hell did that mean? I never threatened her or spoke crossly to her. Granted, I didn't have anything in common with any of the girls on campus, but what was so terrifying about me that my roommate would flee for her life? I shook my head and closed my door. I lay on the bed still holding that blasted book. Inner peace, yeah, right.

By morning, I was actually relieved to have a room all to myself. Christmas vacation was coming up soon and I'd basically have the entire campus to myself. I briefly wondered what Wally was doing over Christmas break, then caught myself, and tried to find something else to think about. I would have to go home for a couple of days, max, but I'd make an excuse and hightail it back here. I wondered what it would be like to go hiking in the mountains over Christmas. I was a kindred spirit with Vera on that point, at least, the mountains brought me peace too.

I went to classes, but I couldn't tell you a danged thing I 'learned'. Just going through the motions. This was Monday, my long day. I wouldn't be able to go home until somewhere around seven o'clock. By the time I got home, I was tired, hungry and cranky. I stripped down and put my flannel pajamas on and still chilly, I grabbed a ratty, moth-eaten sweater. I was getting ready to settle down to read '*how to gain inner peace*' when I noticed a white slip of paper by the door. I gave an exaggerated sigh and stalked over to the door, snatching it up.

Hey, Beautiful, since the ice cream 'date' was a bust, how about meeting me for a milkshake? W.

I shook my head and flopped back on my bed. Just as I opened the book, I heard a tap on the window. Irritated, I went to the window and looked down. Wally stood with his face raised and eyes glued to the window. I opened the window, surprised at how cold the wind was that whooshed through the opened window.

"I'm tired!" I shouted down to him.

"Then you need something for energy. A milkshake would be perfect!" he shouted back.

"I'm reading a book!" I yelled.

"It'll be there when you get back. Come on!" he insisted.

I saw the dorm mother come down the steps at an angry march and shoo him off.

"Wait!" I yelled after him, "Where?"

The dorm mother, I think her name was Margaret, glared up at me.

34

"The patio!" I heard his fading voice reply.

"You aren't to be encouraging this behavior, Miss Sarangowski!" Margret shouted at me with a finger jabbing the air.

"Sorry!" I called down to her.

I dressed quick as lightning and ran down the stairs. Margaret was standing by the door with her arms folded.

"We aren't going to have a repeat performance of the last time you went running off, are we?" she said ominously.

"No, ma'am," I answered.

She gave me one last laser look and stalked off, shaking her head. I heard her mumble under her breath, "And they wonder why I drink."

Wally was dutifully sitting at the patio table bundled up as though he was ice fishing in Antarctica. I could see him shiver from across the patio. Even though he had gloves on, he blew on his hands.

"You know how stupid this is?" I asked as I sat down.

"Anytime is a good time for ice cream," he smiled with chattering teeth.

"Yeah, well, I prefer not to be colder than what I'm drinking," I said nonchalantly.

"Then how about some hot chocolate?" he compromised.

"That would probably be good, providing it doesn't freeze into a fudge pop before we get it drank," I countered.

He laughed and I let a smile slip across my lips.

We stomped inside to the cafeteria where it felt hot compared to outside. We began to shed outerwear and then went to the vending machine for hot chocolate. When we got back to the table, Wally looked around the cafeteria and reached in his coat pocket. He brought out a brown bottle.

"What's that?" I asked.

"Bailey's Irish Crème," he answered with a crooked smile.

"Again. What's that?"

"You've never had Bailey's? Oh, you are in for a treat!"

He poured a dollop in my hot chocolate and I tentatively sipped.

My mouth exploded with a sweetness that even rivaled mom's 'special' cookies! I don't think I'd ever tasted anything so delicious!

"Good, huh?" he chuckled.

"Well, Wally, for once you did something right," I said savoring every sip.

He kept me plied with Bailey's Irish Crème and hot chocolate and we talked about a variety of things. School, we both hated. Parents, we both were pretty ambivalent. He asked how in the world I'd ended up with a name like Probably Magic, and I told him the supposed story between giggles. I was certainly warm now and everything seemed funny.

All at once he stopped and leaned toward me. I thought he was going to kiss me, so I leaned forward too. Instead, he whispered, "You see any guys staring at you this time?"

I reared back, feeling foolish and embarrassed. "Ass!" I hissed at him.

He laughed and then turned semi-serious, "All kidding aside, tell me what's going on with that."

I was shocked that I actually began to talk to him, starting with the boys in the Cadillac to the guy standing behind the fountain. When I finished, I sat running my finger around the rim of the cup bracing myself for the obligatory, "Dang! You *are* weird!"

Instead, I felt him crook a finger under my chin and lift my head.

"I just *knew* there was something very special about you," he said softly.

He smiled at me and I melted. I felt tears fill my eyes. For one thing, it felt good to get it off my chest, to actually say the words aloud, for the second thing, I felt stupid and dirty. I had contaminated a budding friendship and it would never be the same playful banter we had known these past months.

"Red, there are things in this world we don't understand. Experiences that just don't fit neatly into the box we label NORMAL in crayon. I saw your face in both of these instances and I have no doubt whatsoever, you believe them to be real."

I started to protest that last part, but he held up a finger to shush me. "Let me finish. I didn't experience them; I've never experienced anything like that. If and when I do, then it will be as I believe, and I hope you're there with me when I do. So, the best I can do is tell you I believe you."

"Really? Now you're all mature like?" I grumbled.

Wally laughed and so did I. You know what? It felt good to have a friend. Maybe someday I would tell him about the creepy Whispers Bookstore.

Chapter Six

I woke with washed-out sunlight trying to penetrate the clouds. A haze nearly obscured the mountains, then I realized it was snowing up there, a lot! My head felt like a balloon stretched to the limit before exploding. I moaned, threw an arm across my eyes, and turned on my back. My stomach felt like I'd swallowed lead balls and my head throbbed in sync with my pulse. I peeked with one eye at the clock. With an even louder groan, I flopped around on the bed in a mini temper tantrum. I didn't want to go to class! I felt like death warmed over. Maybe I could stay home sick.

I dutifully and responsibly rolled out of bed and made my way down to the shower. I didn't even turn the hot water on, I just let the icy stream try to freeze some sense into me. By the time I'd finished, I felt even worse. I was starving. Breakfast in the cafeteria was over. The vending machines seemed about as inviting as being in the room with a rabid dog. I remembered mom's special cookies. Just what I needed, more sugar, but it was better than nothing.

As I munched the cookies, I began to feel better. Really! I was feeling better! These were mom's special magic cookies! I was even beginning to be in a good mood. Everything moved in slow motion and it looked so funny! I began to laugh and couldn't stop. That wasn't good, I'd gotten in trouble many times for laughing at inappropriate times. I tried to hold back the giggles, but they came out my nose anyway, and I was snorting and then laughing because I was snorting. I picked up my books and made my way to class.

I met Wally on the way. I was so happy to see him!

"Hey, ol' buddy, ol' pal!" I greeted him with a punch on the shoulder. He did a double-take.

"You okay, Red?" he asked.

I laughed because he looked so danged serious. I tried to put a serious look on my face too, but instead, I erupted in laughter, "I'm perfect! Hey! Did you see it snowing on the mountain this morning? Oh, Wally, it was so beautiful! I wanted to run right up there and be in it. Seriously, I want to be a rabbit running through the snow, a white rabbit, on white snow. You know, to camouflage me. There are mountain lions up there, you know, and they like to eat rabbits. Maybe I'll just be a snowy owl. Is there such a thing as a snowy owl? I would be high in the trees..."

"Um, Red, slow down. What is wrong with you?" Wally said taking me by the shoulders and giving me a little shake. He looked deep into my eyes and I saw his eyebrows shoot clear up into his hairline. It was hilarious! I began to laugh again.

"Oh my God!" he cried, "You're high as a kite! Red! You cannot go to class like this!" he said steering me toward the cafeteria.

"High? No, I'm not!" I protested.

"Were you reefin' this morning?" he asked as he sat me down.

"Seeing how I have no idea what that means, I doubt it," I said as though he had just said the stupidest thing I'd ever heard. "I've only had some of the cookies Mom sent me.

Maybe I'm on a sugar high. We had an awful lot of hot chocolate last night," I said giving him an exaggerated wink.

"Red, I think your mom put weed in the cookies," he said still trying to convince me.

I stood up suddenly angry, "MY MOTHER DOES NOT PUT WEEDS IN COOKIES! Granted, she's not the best cook, but everyone loves her cookies!"

Wally snickered and said under his breath, "I bet they do!"

Slowly it began to dawn on me. My eyes opened so wide they should have popped from my head. "Oh, no!"

I sat down again and slumped low in my chair. What if everyone knew I was high on weed? I could get expelled for using drugs! Trying to act normal, I looked even more suspicious.

"Red, it'll wear off in a couple of hours. No more cookies, okay?" he said staring at me with those deep blue eyes, wait, they were more of a hazel, more pond scummy today. In fact, they were beautiful! That dark hazel green with gold flecks dancing in the cafeteria lights. What happened to the beautiful ocean blue? Ocean blue, that was a beautiful name for a color. I guess oceans could look pond scummy too.

"You have beautiful eyes, Wally," I said dreamily.

"Okay, that's it. You're going back to your room and I don't want you going anywhere or talking to anybody. Got it?" he said nervously.

"What if Margaret stops me?" I asked wide-eyed as the implications wormed its way through my foggy brain.

"Just tell her you have a stomach bug or something and you need to go lay down. Don't, I repeat, don't get into a conversation and Red? For the love of Pete, don't start laughing!"

I nodded my head, feeling very much in control. He walked me to my dorm, and I slipped up the stairs and flopped on my unmade bed. Sleep came fast and easy. When I woke a few hours later, the first thing I did was throw away the remainder of the container of mom's cookies. She and I were going to have to have a little chat. Now, all those years of telling me how everyone loved her cookies made sense. No wonder her cookies made them happy. Maybe I should have given them to the bullies in school?

Life slowed down some after the Great Cookie Event. Christmas break was coming fast. Exams were coming even faster. Wally and I studied for hours and hours, sometimes together, sometimes in our own rooms. Christmas break couldn't come fast enough. I was exhausted. Kids began to disappear from campus taking early break, the lawn and the bushes faded from sight, under great mounds of snow. I guess some kids weren't able to leave when planned and while some decided to leave early, some tried to wait out the snow and impassable roads. Colorado was used to this kind of weather and had snow control down to a fine art.

However, the snowstorm provided the perfect cover for me. I was still pretty miffed at my mother. I called home and sounding dutifully disappointed, I explained that everything and everyone was pretty much frozen in place. She and my dad sounded properly disappointed as they pointed out my safety was above all else.

"I'll send you some cookies overnight," Mom promised.

"NO!" I practically yelled. I was not accustomed to yelling at my parents, so I rushed to explain I still had some, thank you.

"Probably, you've been at school for almost four months! Don't you like them?" Mom asked, deeply hurt.

"I love them! Hey, no, Mom, I just ration them out so I can enjoy them more," I lied.

"Well, if you're sure…" she replied knowing full well I was lying.

I was emotionally drained by the time the phone call ended. All that lying was exhausting, but now I was free for two whole weeks! I looked around my tiny room and suddenly felt very alone. It was like being free but still in prison. I wasn't sure what I was going to do by myself.

There was a rap at the door, and I opened it to the scowling face of Margaret.

"I need to know when you're leaving," she grumbled.

"I'm going to stay here," I said.

"What? Staying here?" she practically shouted. "If you stay here then I have to cancel my plans and not go home!"

I had to think fast which, was no easy task. "Stay here…until…until my flight leaves in a couple of hours!" I said pleased with myself. "You meant over the break?" I sniffed and reiterated my lie, "I thought you were talking about now. You meant over the break. Yeah, my plane leaves in about three hours, I'll be leaving then."

"You said two hours," she corrected me suspiciously.

"Two hours, three hours, who knows with this weather, right?" I said cheerfully. Man! I was getting good at this lying thing. Should that be disturbing? I've always been brutally honest, so I was pretty surprised the lies rolled off my tongue so easily.

"Are you lying to me, Miss Sarangoski?" she asked through narrowed eyes.

"Absolutely not!" I emphasized. "Go home and fill up on good eats and egg nog. The real stuff, Margaret, not the sissy stuff."

She had to glare at me for a few seconds to drive home her point, and then said, "If you're absolutely positive." She got a look of concentration which made deep wrinkles in her forehead. "I guess I could put off leaving for a few hours…"

"In this weather? Oh no! If I were you, I'd leave right away!" I said definitely panicked.

"I could drive you to the airport," she said chewing her lower lip.

"Oh, that's so sweet! But I have…a…taxi coming to pick me up. A taxi!" I said feeling the fear begin to set in.

"Oh, well, if you're sure," she finally relented.

A deep sigh of relief escaped me, which I turned into a gesture that perhaps insinuated that I really needed to finish packing.

"I'm sure," I said and began to close the door. She put her hand out to stop it.

"On the other hand," she continued, "what if the flight is delayed or, even worse, canceled?"

"I'll be fine," I promised while fighting the urge to slam the door in her face. "I promise everything will be just fine, as long as I can finish packing."

She peeked inside my room, "You haven't even started yet? You know you have to be at the airport two hours early."

"Truly, Margaret, I've got it under control," I said desperate to get rid of her.

"Well, okay," she put her hand down and allowed me to close the door. I leaned against it and listened to her footsteps fade away. A few minutes later, I heard a car door slam and tires crunching on the frozen slush. I risked a peek out the window and watched her drive away.

FREEDOM! I shouted in my mind.

I heard another tap on the door. Seriously? I'd just watched her drive away! Did she change her mind and come back? I quickly threw a bunch of clothes on the bed, grabbed my suitcase and threw some underwear in, made sure my hair was appropriately messy and answered the door.

There stood Wally with, most likely, the most beautiful girl I'd ever seen.

Chapter Seven

"Wally?" I asked eyeing the girl suspiciously. Was that a little pang of jealousy?

"Merry Christmas, Red! Adriana and I thought we'd stop and say hi. You gonna be okay here by yourself?" he asked.

I stood there dumbfounded and couldn't get any words out of my mouth. I'd never considered Wally might have a girlfriend. Why would he fail to mention something like that?

"Red? You okay?" he asked.

"Would you quit asking me if I'm okay every time you see me?" I barked.

Princess Adriana laughed and touched Wally's arm protectively. "She's exactly as you described her!"

Wally kind of laughed too, "She's one in a million, that's for sure."

"Ummm…I am standing right in front of you. I can hear what you say," I said preparing to close the door in both their faces.

For the second time this morning, a hand shot out and held the door open.

"Awwww…it's Christmas, Red, be nice," he scolded good-naturedly.

"This is my little sister, Adriana. She drove up to help me get packed," he explained.

His sister! Well, come to think of it, she had the same hazel eyes, but how was she so freakin' beautiful?

"Do I call you Red too?" she asked.

I thought about it and finally said, "Sure. Why not?"

"Well, can we come in or do we have to stay in the hall?" Wally said with a smile. "I saw the dorm monster leave. The university is pretty much empty."

"Oh! Sure! Come in," I invited, opening the door wide.

Wally looked at the clothes and suitcase, "Either you got vandalized or you decided to go home after all."

"Nope, I liked to never got rid of Margaret, so I had to pretend I was packing. She was going to cancel her plans if I was staying on campus," I explained.

"But you *are* staying on campus," Adriana pointed out.

"Yeah, but if any student in the dorm doesn't leave, they have to have a chaperone…it's complicated," I stammered.

Wally smiled lovingly at his sister, "It's okay. If anyone can take care of themselves, it's Red."

I wasn't sure if I'd just been complimented or insulted. Before I could decide, Adriana spoke up. "Do you always wear your hair down? It's beautiful! Is that your natural color? I'd love to have my hair that color. It's such a bright…well, red! Is that why my brother calls you Red?"

I was taken aback at the stream of words coming from this little slip of a girl.

"Umm…" I hesitated.

"I could teach you how to braid it if you don't know how. It would be awesome in a braid," she gushed.

"Umm…"

"Wallace, we have time, don't we? It wouldn't take long and then it wouldn't get in her way so much," she hurried on. Apparently, *Wallace* never said no to his sister. He nodded. She turned to me and commanded me to sit on the bed.

"Umm…"

She gave me a gentle push and I dropped onto the bed. Her fingers were quick and nimble. Before I knew it, I was sporting a braid about three inches in diameter and four feet long. It swung heavily down my back.

She swiped around my face and studied her handiwork, "I can't do anything about the curls around your face. They're too short to put in the braid but take a look!"

I stood and looked in the mirror over my dresser. I stared at the face staring back at me. My cheekbones stood out, my mouth was soft and full, my eyes a blazing green. Without that massive mass of hair obscuring my face, I could actually see myself!

"Thank you!" I said to her. She beamed proudly.

"I want to be a beautician," she announced. "I love working with hair. Do you use conditioner? You should really use conditioner; it would help with the flyaways."

"Umm…"

"Don't worry, I have an extra bottle in my suitcase. I'll drop it by before we leave," she promised as she turned to her brother. "We need to go."

Wally stood back looking smugly amused, "Yes, ma'am."

He stepped forward and gave me a peck on the cheek, "Merry Christmas, Red. Please, please, stay out of trouble while I'm gone. I'll be back in about ten days, but I'll call you, okay?"

"I don't have a phone," I informed him.

"Okay, that's your homework during vacation. Go buy a cell phone," he said sternly.

"Okay," I said nodding my head and feeling the heavy braid pulling my head back.

When they left, I just stood by the door. Wow! That was a hurricane-force visit! I blinked as I tried to regain my equilibrium. The braid swung from side to side. The jury was still out on the hairstyle, besides, I'm not sure I could duplicate it.

After Adriana dropped off the promised conditioner, they were finally on their way. I was alone at last. The hall was quiet, the dorm was quiet, the campus was quiet, and the classrooms were quiet. I could see a couple of lights on in the admin building. I figured they would do a final walkthrough before leaving for the holiday, so I dressed warm and decided I would go into town. See what's shaking there.

Not much. The stores were packed with holiday shoppers but without the college students, the streets were pretty quiet. I warily eyed the street where Whispers Bookstore was located. I was still a little leery about going back. I really needed to get the meditation book back to Vera though. I was just going to have to work up my nerve and do it.

I stopped at a small café and ordered breakfast. It was kind of a comfort food thing. Whenever I was bothered by something, it seemed scrambled eggs, biscuits, and gravy, and crispy bacon made the world bearable once again. I decided to treat myself and ordered a slice of cherry pie. I'd gotten used to eating alone in public places, so I was surprised when a woman came to my table and sat down.

"Hi," I said for lack of anything more creative. She said nothing. "Can I help you?" Still silence. Then she just vanished! She was sitting there and then she wasn't. I tried to remember details about her and was frustrated because I couldn't. Blonde? Gray? Young? Old? Oh no! Not this again! The table next to mine had a young couple holding hands. They were staring at me, all while trying not to be obvious about it.

"Poor thing," the woman whispered, "My heart goes out to the homeless people. So many of them have a degree of mental illness. They talk to themselves a lot. Are they speaking to voices in their head or just for company?" She looked at her companion and leaned in, "And at Christmas! My heart is breaking!"

"I'm not homeless, and I can hear you! You might want to work on the volume of your whispering," I protested.

The woman blushed deeply and lowered her eyes.

"I'm not! I'm a student at the University of Colorado!" my voice raising an octave.

"Now, see what you've done?" the boyfriend hissed. "They're unpredictable and when they get upset, you just never know what they're going to do! Let's go."

He hurriedly threw money on the table and with an arm protectively around the woman's waist, he propelled her out the door.

"I'm not HOMELESS!" I shouted after them.

Well, that took the festivity out of my cherry pie. I left it untouched and left the diner. I could feel my face burning. Who was my visitor anyway? Another, more urgent question came to mind, why am I all of a sudden seeing these mysterious apparitions? Besides, weren't ghosts supposed to be these filmy, see-through'y things? Was I turning into my Aunt Jo? People already whispered about me, now, I suppose, they'll start having those intervention discussions about what mental hospital to check me into. I was feeling pretty depressed. Nothing to do but to go back to my room and pout.

As I pulled into the driveway with the gate, a man in a uniform stepped out. George the security guard! My heart thudded heavily against my chest. I'd forgotten all about security staying on the grounds during the holiday.

I pulled up to him and lowered my window. "Hi, George!"

"Hey, Probably. What are you doing here?" George asked.

"I, uh, I…" I couldn't even think of a plausible lie. "George, I'm going to be honest with you."

"Okay," he said as he settled in for the certain yarn I was about to spin. He placed a hand on the roof of the car and looked in the window with a smug smirk.

"I'm staying here during the holiday. I don't want to go home. I don't want to go anywhere. I want to stay here and relax and recharge. I need to be alone."

George nodded his head and then looked over the top of the car. "You're not supposed to be here without supervision."

"I know," I said too weary to argue.

"Well, okay. I'll be checking on you and if you need anything, call me," he said and waved me on.

But I don't have a cell phone! I thought to myself.

Chapter Eight

Darkness came early. Between the massive dark clouds, the mountains, and my mood, there wasn't much chance any sunlight would filter through. I was exhausted. It had been a very busy day and lying constantly was exhausting. I briefly wondered if George was possibly an ally or if he just didn't want to rock the boat and have even more to answer for, so he let me go. I thought the braid might make me less formidable, less hard-edged, but maybe my hardness was already hardwired into people after meeting me.

I walked down the hall, looking forward to a nice hot shower, not having to share any hot water with the girls on the floor. In fact, I could take a shower here, run down to the second floor and take a shower there, and then to the first floor. I loved to feel the heat pounding down on me. It seeped into my bones thawing me, making me warm at last. The braid was even heavier when it was wet. Finally, I was satisfied and stepping out, I took my towel and wiped the steam from the mirror. On an impulse, I just carried my towel and walked buck naked to my room. Take that, Margaret!

I dressed for bed and got under the covers. Something hard was poking into my back. I turned the bedside lamp on and got out of bed to inspect. It was the book on meditation. Weird. Why would I throw this book on the bed? Perhaps in the heat of the moment when I pretended to be packing? Who knew? I was busy trying to think of a lie for the lie of the lie…oh, forget it. It's complicated. Just to humor my freedom, I opened the book and began to read. I looked at the clock and figured I'd just read for fifteen minutes or so. Less if it proved to be as boring as I suspected. It was 10:30. Plenty of time to at least put in the effort.

I looked at the clock again. 12:30 AM? Impossible! I picked up the clock and shook it. Stupid thing must be on the fritz. Okay, buy a cell phone and a clock. Dang! I got out of bed and went downstairs to the kitchenette hoping there was at least a little something to eat or drink. I walked into the gathering room and just glanced at the wall clock. 12:45 AM. Suddenly, I wasn't hungry or thirsty. I backed out of the room and ran up the stairs to my room and slammed the door. Curiouser and curiouser.

I felt the hair on my arms stand to attention as the goosebumps raised. I slipped into bed and turned the light off. Could I have really read for two straight hours? I looked at the page I'd turned down. It was in the middle of the book. I eventually went to sleep but it was a restless, fitful sleep.

My eyes opened but it was difficult to see. A moonless night made it black with only the reflection of the snow casting any light at all. I stared at the ceiling for a while. As tired as I was, I wondered what would wake me up. Too much going on in my mind. It was just churning with questions, thoughts, and worries. I turned on my side and that's when I saw the man standing in my room!

I quickly rolled out of bed and got caught in the covers, landing on my shoulder. The pain streaked right to my head. I kicked the covers free and grabbed the closest weapon I could find, my Totes soft as a cloud house slipper. I flopped it at the man and screamed, "Who are you and what are you doing in my room?"

He didn't say anything. I crab-walked to the nightstand and reached behind me to turn on the light. The room was empty. I checked the closet. Empty. I checked the door. Locked. No wet or muddy footprints. I nervously laughed as I saw my parka hanging on the back of the door. *You really are losing your mind*, I laughed at myself. Still giggling, I crawled back into bed and turned off the light. I turned to my side once again…and there he was.

Out of bed again and this time a little more dignified. I raised my other slipper at him, "Don't come any closer or I will rip your arm off and beat you with it!"

The man put his hand inside his coat, and I threw the slipper at him. It thudded softly on the door behind him, as only memory foam can do. He watched it come at him and then watched as it passed right through him and landed on the door. He withdrew his hand and held out an envelope.

"What?" I shouted at him. It then occurred to me; he was dressed oddly. I carefully sidestepped a little closer. What I saw brought me up short. He was wearing a Civil War Uniform, complete with a cap. His face looked so sad and so desperate. Not threatening, just sad. I stepped a little closer to his outstretched hand. I began to see he was a bit see-through. I waved my hand at his chest area and my hand passed right through with no more than a cold feeling. I was looking at a genuine, certifiable, ghost! He looked at the envelope and then at me.

"They have mail service in the afterlife?" I asked. He shook his head and stretched out his hand even further.

I looked down and saw calligraphy. It was addressed to Rosa Hargate. "What about it?" I asked. "What do you want me to do with it?"

He dropped his head in mourning. I took the letter from his hand. "You want me to read it? Why on earth can't you talk to me? Oh, never mind, you aren't of this earth, are you? Sorry, I'm kinda new at this," I said my heart breaking at his sadness.

"You want me to read it?" I asked again. He raised his head and slowly nodded, then he got lighter and lighter until he was as see-through as vapor and then he was gone.

I stood holding the letter, pretty sure it was just a dream. I laid it on my nightstand and sat on the edge of the bed just considering what a spectacular dream it had been. I really should be writing these things down. They would make a great book one day!

I crawled back into bed and closed my eyes. I kept seeing that poor man's tortured heart though. I wanted to cry for him, and I never cried, for anyone, or anything. Crying was a sign of weakness and being weak was never a luxury I could afford. Eventually, my eyes did close and concluded my night with no more fantastical dreams.

Morning came and I took advantage of my freedom by curling my toes, stretching and yawning, and scratching my belly, all while still in bed. I smiled. I could get used to this! I remembered that weird dream I had. I sat on the edge of the bed and threw my braid back over my shoulder. The braid was good for the daytime, but it was like sleeping on a nautical rope at night. I put my feet down to slide into my slippers, but they weren't there.

I saw one slipper by the door and the other dropped at the foot of the bed. The memory of throwing it at the door tickled the edge of my wakefulness. Frowning, I was almost afraid to look at the nightstand. I glanced, then closed my eyes and shook my head. When I opened my eyes, the envelope still lay in the place I put it last night. I stared at it a few minutes torn as to what I should do. I was wishing Wally was there to verify that, *yes, indeed, Red, there most definitely is a letter on your nightstand.* Or, *what letter? You seeing things again?* Another thought came to me. I'd seen TV shows where objects reportedly could open portals to the "other side" and who knew what could slither into our world? I inched a little closer to the letter and craned my neck to get a good look at it.

There were spots on it. Curiosity drew me closer, that and the fact I'm nosy. I quickly jumped back though. Those were blood spots! A lot of them! I wasn't sure I should touch the envelope or not. On the other hand, I don't think they had HIV in those days and besides, the blood would be over two hundred years old. Pretty sure any kind of bad thing was long gone. Still…

I found a couple of oven mitts my mother had sent me in hopes I might settle down and maybe do normal things, like baking, for example. I'm sure she was hoping one day I would ask for her recipe for her special cookies. I wasn't the Suzie Home Baker type though. It would never happen. Sorry, Mom. Though it took some clumsy maneuvering, I finally got the envelope opened and drew out a two-page letter. The blood had a faded look as it had soaked into the paper. Rough manuscript filled the pages. I sat there on the edge of the bed, wearing flannel pajamas and oven mitts and read this very personal letter.

Chapter Nine

My dear, Rosa,
July 1, 1863

    I'm sure you're wondering why you are receiving this letter.

    It's kind of a long explanation but I hope you will bear with me as I try to explain. As you know, I got enlisted in the Confederate Army. I'm not sure how this is all going to Turn out yet. The fighting is reel bad and I've seen a lot of

    Death. The Confederates are doing good, but the Unions are not backing down. I know that's not a proper thing to say to such a fine Lady as you are, but it's the truth. It makes a man think about Life and death and how many times we should have done something and didn't. And how many times we should have said something and stayed silent.

    I was remembering two summers past when I saw you at the church Picnic. You was the purttiest thing I'd ever laid eyes on. In fact, You were so purty that I couldn't get the words off my tongue.

    I just kept watching you, amazed at how graceful you were.

    Rosa, I swear the sun traveled clear across the sky just so it could shine on your face. Then when I seed you in town,

    No matter what I was doing, I'd just stop and watch you.

*****

I was at the bottom of the page and quickly brought out the second page.

*****

(2)

Anyway, one of those things I should have said and stayed silent. I fell in love with you the first time I saw you.

You was always kind and even said hello to me one time!

I just dreamed after that one day, you would be saying that To me all the time. If I had eternity with you, it still wouldn't Be long enough. I'd still beg for one more day. This brings me to the should have done things except, I'm doing this one.

Rosa, if I git out of this war alive, would you marry me?

I will spend the rest of my life proving to you that my heart Cannot beat without you, nor would it want to.

I'm gittin ready to post this. They tell me we have a major skirmish tomorrow morn at Cemetery Ridge. Mail is kind of hit and miss Out here, but it doesn't matter when you get this. The question Is the same. Would you consider being my beautiful bride?

If I don't make it out this alive, I'm praying this letter will be taken off my dead body and sent to you. Just know, alive or dead, you are and always will be my one true love.

Love,
Peter Euclid

*****

New smudges appeared on the page. I put a hand to my face and felt tears on my cheeks. What a beautiful love letter! Poor Peter! Did he and Rosa never see each other again? Did he not get the chance to spend the rest of his days proving how much he loved her? And more importantly, the letter was friggin' two hundred years old! Didn't ghosts run into each other running around all willy-nilly in the afterlife? Surely they would have crossed paths sooner or later! Two hundred years was a long time to hunt for a loved one! What did he expect me to do?

I carefully placed the letter back in the envelope. The return address simply said Peter Euclid/Confederate Army/Cemetery Ridge, Pennsylvania. The address simply said Rosa Hargate/Charleston, South Carolina.

Chapter Ten

The next few days were torture. I wanted to help the two lovers find each other, but I didn't know how or even where to begin. Peter had not presented himself since that one night. I began to wonder if it wasn't another one of those weirdly life-like dreams, except, I had the letter. I could hold it in my hands. I could smell the musty age that permeated it. It was as real as the cup that held my vending machine coffee.

What must it be like to love so deeply? How terrified was Peter, that he knew death may very well beckon him from his mission? How heartbreaking to lay dying and the only hope you have, is that someone will find the letter and send it on? He died never knowing.

I decided it was time to visit Miss Vera at Whispers Bookstore again. This time I was prepared for her odd ways. I knew what to expect. Perhaps she would have some idea where I could start.

I tucked the letter in my coat pocket and crunched my way out to the parking lot. The sky was an amazing deep blue with a glaring sun. Here and there, snow and ice twinkled like diamonds scattered on a jeweler's cloth. My breath vapor preceded me, puffing out bigger clouds as I made my way across the lot to my car.

I started it up and let the engine run a bit before engaging and backing out of the space. I'm telling you these details because I did it all automatically without one single thought. My mind was churning with possibilities, questions, and hope. What if Peter never made another appearance? What if I could not find Rosa's family? How was I supposed to deliver a letter to a ghost?

I parked closer to the bookstore; it was just too damned cold to walk three blocks like the first time I visited. I grabbed the meditation book and stomped the snow from my boots as I knocked on the door.

The door opened and there was Vera with the same sunny smile. She seemed very happy I was there.

"Oh, my! What a lovely surprise! What brings you back, Probably?" she practically crowed.

I felt gooseflesh again. Had I told her my name? I didn't remember telling her my name. I must have told her my name when I took the book. I shook my head in my mind, uncertain of anything anymore.

"I brought the book back," I told her while holding the book on meditation out to her.

She frowned, "Awww…you didn't like it?"

"Oh, No! It was very interesting!" I said with a certain amount of guilt. I had not read all of it and didn't remember what I did read the night Peter showed up.

She looked at me with those piercing blue eyes letting me know she knew I was lying.

Hurrying on to change the subject, I asked her about history books.

"Well, my dear," she began, "history has been around for billions of years! You'll need to be a little more specific." She laughed that sweet laugh.

I felt myself blush, "About the Civil War. More specifically, the battle at Cemetery Ridge in Pennsylvania." There. That should be specific enough.

She shook her head and tut-tutted with her tongue, "A very sad and costly battle, that one. The Confederate Army had been enjoying many successes over the Union Army. The Union Army got wise to the Confederate strategy and in a bloody sweep of Cemetery Ridge, the Confederates were defeated. Very sad how many men lost their lives in that battle. Are you doing a paper for school on the Civil War?"

Okay, how did she know I was a student?

She took me by the hand and sat me on the sofa where I sat last time.

"Something is troubling you, my dear. Would you like to talk about it?" she asked softly.

"I find it very difficult to talk to people about things," I confessed.

"I tell you what, I was just getting ready to enjoy a cinnamon roll and a cup of tea. So good on a blustery day like today! Would you care to join me? We can go into the kitchen if you like. It's nice and warm in there," she invited.

I found myself nodding and feeling like I really did want to talk to someone about this. I was in over my head and Miss Vera seemed very non-judgmental. After all, would a person who had certain strict restrictions carry a book on genitalia tattooing? Or the one I saw about black magic/white magic? Her books ran from one extreme to the other and somewhere in the middle, there were books for normal people.

We sat at an old wooden table. I could tell it had been lovingly cared for and well used for many, many years. Most likely passed down from generation to generation. Vera carefully put two cinnamon rolls out and poured tea in delicate china cups. She opened a jar of home-canned strawberries and a tiny silver spoon to dip them out. She sat and folded her hands in front of her.

"Talk to me," she coaxed me.

I took the letter from my pocket and slid it over to her. She looked at it with interest and I nodded permission for her to read it. I watched her eyes go from line to line and then her hand flutter to cover her heart. I saw the tears in her eyes.

She gently lay the letter between us and sat silent for a moment.

"Where did you get such a beautiful letter?" she asked.

"From Peter Euclid," I said without fanfare.

"I had a sneaking suspicion you were one of those," she said with the barest of smiles.

"One of what?" I asked feeling my hackles rise.

"Probably, there are people who have a beautiful gift. Most people don't understand, they fear the unknown and so they close themselves off to the vast world we live in. They're content to just live among their familiar, never stepping beyond the walls they construct. Then there are people who are open to the possibilities, the unexplained, the *abnormal* if you will. Your name may have been a precursor to being able to be aware of beings not of this world."

I felt a need to correct her, "I didn't ask for this. I've never experienced anything like this before. Hell, I mean, heck, I don't even believe in ghosts! Besides, what does he want me to do with this?" My fingertip lightly tapped the envelope.

"Evidently he has great trust in you. I think he wants you to find Rosa and finally let her know how much she was loved," Vera said before sipping her tea.

"How could he feel anything toward me? He doesn't and never did know me," I reasoned.

"Oh, Probably, my dear, your gift is so rare, so delicate, so cherished, they find you," Vera said the tears returning to her eyes.

I told her about the boys in the Cadillac. When I'd finished, she nodded her head, "I remember that night. I wasn't much more than a young teen myself."

"You *knew* them?"

"Well, I didn't *know* them," she explained. "We ran in much different social circles at the time. I believe the boy you saw was named Chuck Doup? Maybe Chuck Day? Something like that. His parents had just bought him that Cadillac. All shiny new from the showroom floor. Back in those days, if you had a brand new car, you attracted the attention of everyone. Those that admired it, and those who envied it.

Rocco Tempe was the town bad boy. He swaggered and bullied his way to a standing in our little town until everyone was afraid of him. Well, he started hanging out with Chuck and you could see the change begin to come over Chuck. He smoked cigarettes, his language sneaked in colorful words, he just began to change. Rocco had a plan though. It was important to him to stay top dog and some squeaky-clean kid with a brand new Cadillac wasn't going to dethrone him."

I sat enthralled by the story. Miss Vera sure knew how to spin a tale! "What happened?" I urged her to continue.

"Well, Rocco challenged Chuck to a drag race," she began.

"Uh oh, I'm afraid I know how this all turns out," I interrupted.

"So, who's telling the story, you or me?" she said blue eyes flashing.

"I'm sorry," I apologized, "Please, do go on. I really do want to hear the story."

"Well, it had been raining all day and Chuck was thinking surely the race would be called off. Sometimes Fate can be very cruel, Probably," the old woman said shaking her head. "It quit raining just as the sun went down. Chuck hadn't heard from Rocco, so he made plans with his friends. It was deep summer, and everything was washed clean. Chuck and his friends went to the local drive-in, I seem to recall it was called Archie's Park-N-Eat back then. It's been long gone now. Archie was forever running the teenagers off. They didn't come to eat; they came to socialize with other teenagers.

Well, the boys were goofing around as young boys do. Chuck put down the top on the Cadillac and they had a great time hassling the pretty girls and talking guy stuff. Rocco never showed. Chuck would never admit he was relieved, but he was. It was getting late and Archie came out and made them all leave. Chuck and his crew started the journey home.

They got about halfway home when headlights came racing up behind them. The car would almost touch their bumper! Then it would slow way down, then race up to them again."

"Was it Rocco?" I asked realizing I'd been holding my breath.

Vera gave me 'the look' and I sat leaning forward and made the gesture for shutting up now.

"Now, where was I?" she pondered.

"The car kept playing tag with them," I said helpfully.

"Oh, yes, now I remember," she said as she continued on. "All at once, the car came up beside them and began to crowd them. Their tires slipped off the pavement and mud sprayed. They yelled at the driver and flipped him the finger. The car fell way back, so far back, they couldn't see the headlights. They were nearly home, going around the last bend in the road. As they rounded the bend, suddenly there were headlights in front of them! Coming straight for them! Chuck slammed on the brakes and the car fishtailed, left the road, and went straight into a rain-swollen river."

I sat waiting for the conclusion, bug-eyed.

"Yeah, yeah, so what happened?" I urged her to finish.

Vera shrugged her shoulders, "No one knows. They were never found."

I sat back in my chair, "Didn't they check the river?"

"Many times," the old woman nodded.

"What about the riverbanks when the water receded?" I asked.

Vera merely nodded, "Nothing. They were never seen again. Four young teenage boys just vanished. Oh, people looked for them for years and even now, every once in a while, you'll see a blurb in the newspaper where someone thinks they saw the old car, but it's never panned out. They have been and still remain, just gone."

I felt oddly unsatisfied. Was Chuck like Peter in that he had unfinished business too? Because they vanished into thin air, was that why the car and the boys vanished right in front of my eyes?

I looked at Vera with pleading eyes, "Miss Vera, am I going crazy?"

Vera smiled and patted my hand, "Honey, define crazy."

Well, that wasn't helpful at all!

I slumped in my chair and noticed a book laying on the table. The book title was *Navigating Through Genealogy*. I sat back a little and looked at her. "Where did this come from?"

She only smiled. I was 100% sure I had not brought the book into the kitchen with me. How could it be about genealogy, a subtle hint of where I needed to start to find Rosa?

"Something is nagging at me," I said. May as well get it all out.

"What is that, dear?"

"How did you know my name was Probably?"

She smiled, "Well, you must have told me!"

I was pretty sure I hadn't, and I got that feeling I was walking on an Earth that was tilted off its axis.

"Let's find that book on the Civil War you wanted," she said helpfully as she put our cups and saucers in the sink.

Chapter Eleven

The days passed and Christmas break was coming to a close. Wally would be back tomorrow. Peter had not shown himself and once again I began to wonder if I was losing my mind. The genealogy actually proved very interesting and helpful, but by afternoon, my eyes were tired, and my brain was shutting down. I looked out my window at the mountains and felt a great longing to be up there. I wanted the snow and the quiet. I dressed warmly and struggled into my fur-lined boots. On my way out of the gate, I let George know where I was going. I gave him a time I would try to return and went merrily on my way. We had a great understanding and had gained a mutual respect for one another.

I got to the parking area at the trailhead with some difficulty. The park maintenance crew tried really hard to keep the parking lot reasonably clear for tourists with a great sense of adventure and those who had no sense at all. I figured I fell somewhere in that last category. I took one more deep breath of the warm air in the car and got out. I immediately fell on my butt. My teeth clacked together, and the air left my lungs with a loud grunt. I had a hard time getting my footing, with feet splaying in opposite directions and me holding on to the door handle for dear life. After quite a show of acrobatic prowess, I was finally able to stand. I didn't trust my footing, traction boots or not, and hobbled trying to hold onto the car as I slid my way to the trail.

Once I was in snow, mobility greatly increased. I surveyed my surroundings and realized I was in the Colorado Mountains alone. Yeah, definitely in the second category of having no sense at all. I began walking the familiar trail, or at least I thought so. Other than rabbit tracks, most likely bear tracks, and something I hoped wasn't a hungry mountain lion, the trail was undisturbed. I couldn't tell exactly where it was, but every once in a while, there would be a bare patch where the heavy evergreens caught the snow before it found the ground. I was so intent on trying to stay on track, I didn't realize just how far I'd gone. I brushed snow off a fallen log and sat down.

I don't know if you've ever been in the mountains when they're covered with snow, but you should, at least once in your lifetime. The air feels almost solid, the noises amplified yet muted. You almost expect an echo, but the air is so crystalline, it stops any further noise. I heard noises I could not identify, and I have to admit it made my heart beat a little faster. I heard familiar noises like the caw of the crows, the tapping of the woodpecker, falling acorns as squirrels scampered back to their warm nests. I listened to the gentle shoosh-shoosh as a small animal scratched in the snow and the cry of a small puppy.

Wait! What? A puppy? Up here in the snow alone? I jumped to my feet and tried to zero in on the direction. It meant leaving the trail, or what I thought was the trail, but the poor thing would freeze to death out here alone! How could I live with myself knowing I'd left a baby…of any kind…to take its chances in this brutal weather? I'd walk a few steps then stop and listen. A few more steps and listen. I was getting closer; the puppy was sounding weaker. I hurried as fast as I could through the thorned brambles and heavy undergrowth. The ground swelled and dipped, and I alternated falling to my knees and falling on my butt.

The cries stopped. So did I. I listened hard but all I could hear was the other woodland noises.

"Shut. Up!" I shouted. I wish I could tell you everything went quiet, but it didn't. In fact, a squirrel was apparently upset being yelled at and hit me with an acorn. I am pretty sure that rodent was aiming for me. He managed to ping me three or four times before I began picking up acorns and throwing them back at him. I covered my head with my arms and took off running to get out of his range. I'm sure we were both glaring at each other, but I could no longer see him. *What kind of maniac gets into a fight with a squirrel?* My mind inquired. "Shut up," I muttered, "he started it."

A pitiful little whine caught my ear. It was very close now. I moved some heavy pine branches and saw a gray river slicing through the snow. Huge boulders stood out of the water like sentries. Icicles clung to low hanging branches and the backflow of the water, trying to round the rocks, was a cold, glassy, green. The river was deep and swift and very, very cold. There on the boulder, in the middle of the river, sat a small, frightened puppy. He lay against sticks and river debris caught between two rocks. I could see him shivering from where I was standing. My heart went out to him. I didn't know how to get to him though. He looked at me with pleading eyes and stood up, as if to say, "You've come to rescue me! I'm going to be okay now!" The puppy began pawing the rock and acting like he was going to jump in the river to get to me.

72

"No!" I screamed, "Stay there! I'll come to you!" Like I thought he could understand what I was shouting at him, or that I could even get to him.

I quickly scanned the riverbank and saw a path leading to the water about three yards upriver. I paid no mind to the limbs whipping in my face and stinging my frozen cheeks. I got to the path and...Damn that water looks cold! The puppy whined again. I took a deep breath and plunged in.

All my winter gear made me heavy and as the swift current carried me downstream, I bobbed up and down, underwater, up for a breath, underwater, up for a breath. I finally felt my body slam into the rocks. I tried to grab hold of anything to stop my downward surfing. My fingers were beyond frozen, I didn't seem to have any strength. The puppy and I both were going to drown, and no one would know to look for us here. We would vanish from the face of the earth like Chuck and his Cadillac.

I felt a flush spread throughout my frozen body. The intense cold was replaced with a warm, cozy feeling. I saw me sitting in Vera's kitchen, the smell of fresh cinnamon rolls, the woodstove radiating welcomed heat. I noticed the tiny blue Forget-Me-Nots painted at the very rim of the thin china cups. I could see the steam rising from the tea, I was acutely aware of the pop, and fizzle of the water cooling in the tea kettle. I wanted to sink into all the warmth and comfort of Vera's kitchen.

I opened my eyes and I was laying on the riverbank. The puppy was curled up inside my coat. He was exhausted and sleeping with the happy twitching of a warm, rescued baby. I carefully sat up, taking care not to disturb him too much. My clothes were dry, and fire danced two feet in front of me. I shook my head. Did I start a fire? I had read somewhere that when one starts to freeze to death, they get very warm. That's why so many times, freezing victims are found with no clothes on or their outerwear discarded. Had we frozen to death and this was the euphoria that comes with dying?

I heard a motorized whine somewhere above me. I sat still, not sure what to do. I heard crunching as heavy boots, then heavy breathing made its way down the hill to the riverbank. I slowly raised my eyes to a man dressed in a green uniform and heavy green coat and gloves.

"It's illegal to have a fire in the park without a permit. You got a permit?" he scowled.

I dumbly shook my head but opened my coat and showed him the puppy. I saw his features soften.

"All dogs are supposed to be on a leash," he continued but I could tell he wasn't nearly as annoyed as he was when he first found me.

"I got lost," I said softly, using my finger to softly pet the puppy's tiny head.

"Of course you did. I can give you a ride back to the guest parking area."

"That would be wonderful," I accepted not taking my eyes off my tiny charge.

"What's your name?" he asked.

I thought of a lifetime of defending my name. I was so disoriented, exhausted, and numb, I just didn't have the strength to do it one more time. Not today, not now.

"Everyone calls me Red."

"Red?"

"Yeah," I took off my hood and my toboggan and that huge, snarled mass of angry red frizz sprang to life.

He smiled and then laughed. He kicked snow over the small fire and made sure it was completely extinguished. He jerked his head toward the snowmobile, "Well, then, come on, Red. I'll get you back to your car."

We rode in silence with the occasional *UMPH!* as we sailed over fallen logs and hidden rocks. I was amazed at just how far I'd gotten off the trail. It truly is a wonder we didn't freeze to death up here. The fire saved our lives. I still didn't remember making a fire. I didn't remember getting to land from the middle of the river and I certainly didn't remove my clothes and dry them before putting them back on. Again, life was getting curiouser and curiouser.

I found out the ranger's name was Bradley. He deposited me right by the driver's side door and then waited as I heated the car. I rolled down my window letting all the hot air out, "Thanks, Ranger Bradley."

"You're welcome. You gonna be okay getting back into town, Red?" he asked, and I could tell he was genuinely concerned.

"Yeah, piece of cake. It's all downhill from here," I smiled and waved as I pulled out of the parking lot.

The last I ever saw of Ranger Bradley was him zooming down the trail until the woods swallowed him up.

I made my way down the slick mountain road. It didn't seem this bad going up. We finally reached the bottom and though I really, really wanted to go home and feel normal, I had nothing for a puppy to eat. I continued past the university and on into town. I stopped at a little convenience store just as the guy was getting ready to flip the Open sign to Closed. I bolted out of the car and ran to the door. It was a race against each other, him trying to get the sign flipped and me trying to gain custody of the door before he did. I won. He was a sore loser.

He followed me around banging the bottom shelves with his broom, sighing unnecessarily loud, and hovering over my shoulder.

"Can I help you find something, miss?" he finally asked, clearly hoping I would just leave.

Instead, I'd had about enough of his wheezy, corn dog grease smell and picked up an air filter and said, "Why yes! Here it is! I came out in this arctic air, traveled dangerously slick roads, risked life and limb to come to this little Podunk store which you protect with an iron fist, to buy this here air filter because I got to thinking, I might want to work on my car!"

"Ha. Ha." He mocked me. "I get it, you're a real comedienne. I need to close up before dark, so if I can help you find something, fine. Otherwise, it's time to vamoose, lady."

"I'm guessing you were awarded Mr. Congeniality at the last Pig-N-Poke conference. Am I right? I'm right, aren't I?" I shot back at him. I grabbed a can of dog food and marched up to the register.

His mood wasn't any better taking my money and he all but pushed me to the door. He pushed open the door, gave me a fake smile and said, "Y'all come back and see us, heah?"

"I really hope there's an online survey about this place," I muttered as I walked to the car and yanked the door open, glaring at him.

Chapter Twelve

Getting the puppy past George was no problem. As I came through the gate, he asked me how the hike went.

"Oh, fine," I replied, not wanting to get in a lengthy conversation with him. It was cold and he wanted to go back into the heated guardhouse as much as I wanted him to just go back to playing Solitaire or whatever they do for endless hours with nothing to do.

He waved me through, and I found my usual parking space, gathered up the puppy and went into the dorm. Once I got to my room, I found an old box Mom had sent goodies in and placed a towel in the bottom. I put the puppy in, and he stood up, looking at me, wagging his little tail.

"I don't think you should get too used to being here," I told him. "Once everyone starts coming back, I won't be able to hide you. Don't worry though, I'll find a great home for you. You hungry?"

I fixed a little bowl of the canned food and put it in the box with him. His tummy became round and tight. Satisfied and exhausted, he climbed out of the box, crawled on my lap and went to sleep. I don't care who you are when a puppy climbs on your lap and snuggles, you don't disturb him. So, I sat there on the floor Indian style and…what could I be doing while this little guy slept? I could see the genealogy book on the bed. I tried to reach for it, but it was just beyond my fingertips. I tried to scoot on my butt ever so careful, but it still was just out of reach.

There was nothing to do, so I just sat there staring at the sparse furnishings, the cover of dust, scattered shoes, and decided I'd make a terrible mom. I didn't even want to know what lurked under the bed.

All at once, the puppy stood up, ears cocked forward, a tiny whine in his throat. He kept looking toward the door.

"What is it?" I asked him. "Were you having a bad dream? Don't worry, little man, you're safe now. I will never let anything hurt you."

He pranced on my legs and continued to stare at the door. He whined and slipping and stumbling, got off my numb legs and trotted to the door.

"You have to go potty?" I asked.

I stood up and began to once again dress for the North Pole and turned off the bedside lamp. When I turned around, there stood Peter Euclid at the door. I jumped like I was shot. The puppy, however, was overjoyed to see him.

"Geez!" I exclaimed, "Peter, you have got to quit doing that!"

He looked at me and slightly smiled. So, he did understand me! His face had a look of hope.

"I haven't made any headway yet, Peter, but I'm working on it. It isn't easy to track down someone who's been dead for over two hundred years with very little to go on," I complained. The truth was, I was still thinking all these things were figments of my imagination, so I didn't make it a priority. Maybe, I should change my thinking.

Peter reached down and gently touched the puppy's head. A smile played across his face. I wondered why he was so lonely. Surely there were other ghosts he had more in common with. Heck, there was good ol' Chuck, he could pal around with, he seemed like a party boy.

When I raised my eyes from the puppy, Peter was gone. The puppy pranced back over to me and seemed disappointed his little bed of warm, long legs was gone.

I sighed and looked at him looking up at me expectantly, "Okay. We started to go out to potty, I guess we should continue." Too late. Tiny little turds trailed behind him and then he stepped in it, so now there were tiny little poopy paw prints dancing across the floor.

"Damnit!" I scolded. Oh, who was I kidding? He was a baby, probably the first human contact he'd ever had. He didn't understand, at least not yet.

He gave a huge yawn. *Yeah, I feel ya, pupper,* I thought. I was pretty whupped myself. I cleaned up his mess and put him back into the box. I got ready for bed and slid between the sheets. I punched the pillow and pulled the covers tight around me. You ever have one of those times when everything was positively perfect? Pillow just right, bed just right, blankets nice and warm? You feel like you could stay just like this forever. My eyes blinked maybe once before I could feel sleep overtake me.

The puppy whined. I didn't move, hoping he would lay down and go to sleep.

He whined again. Then began to sing the song of his people. He crescendoed and passion took over. I put the pillow over my head. Oh, now the puppy howling was starting. I kicked the covers off and stood towering over the box. The puppy looked as far up as his little neck would let him and wagged his tail. He jumped at the side of the box. I felt my heart melting and all common sense leave me. I picked him up and put him in bed with me. He snuggled in the hollow of my neck and promptly went to sleep. The pillow was now all wrong, my pajamas were twisted around me and the covers were too hot. Sleep took a while to visit long enough to close my eyes.

The next morning, I woke with a kink in my neck. I felt feverish and irritable. Puppy was cuddled down in my pillow above my head. Painfully, I got out of bed. Maybe a hot shower would help. I got my stuff together to go down the hall to the shower. Puppy stood up on the bed and wagged his tail.

"No, you don't want to go shower with me," I told him, "You stay here."

Oh, for crying out loud! He was pouting! I wasn't so sure I was cut out to be a dog mom. He looked at me with those cloudy blue eyes and peed on the bed.

"Puppy!" I yelled. Something told me, life had forever changed. It wasn't the parade of ghosts and weird unexplained things happening to me that changed my life, it was a little three-pound ball of fur that changed it. I put him on the floor and he happily trotted behind me down the hall and into the shower. One thing was for sure, I wasn't going to be able to keep him in the dorm room. Which left me two choices, I could both drop out of school and get an apartment, or I could find him a home. Neither one held more good points than bad. We had a history now. I was already in love.

Later in the morning, I was perusing the delectable delicacies of the vending machine for breakfast while my bed linens washed in the Student Laundry. Should I have that prune Pop Tart? Or perhaps the Fire Roasted Doritos? I decided to go into town and get a proper breakfast.

I felt arms go around me. Instinctively, I grabbed onto one arm, twisted, and flipped my assailant over my shoulder.

He landed with a thud, and I straddled him with a fist raised for some serious damage.

"GEEZ, RED! Are you friggin' crazy?" Wally looked up at me with eyes begging for mercy.

"Wally?" I said surprised with fist still raised.

"Could you put your fist down? You're making me nervous and afraid for my life, woman!"

I looked at my fist as though seeing it for the first time. I quickly lowered it and stood, offering him a hand to help him up.

He stood looking amazed, "Where'd you learn to fight like that?"

I gave him an irritated look, "If you were me, you'd learn too. It's come in pretty handy through the years. What are you doing here?"

He had a look of utter confusion on his face. Slowly he enunciated, "I live here. I told you I'd be back before New Year's."

"Oh. Yeah. What day is it anyway?"

"Hey, you don't really want this crap, do you? Let me take you to breakfast. You're obviously going stir crazy being alone all this time," he offered as he took my hand and led me out of the cafeteria.

I left the puppy in my room. What could a tiny puppy do anyway? I failed to mention my new roommate to Wally. I'm not sure why. I just didn't even think of it.

Over a breakfast fit for a queen, I told Wally about my visitors and what I found out about the boys and the Cadillac. I told him of Peter's appearance. He wanted to know who Peter was. It suddenly hit me, so much had happened in the past three weeks, that it would be nearly impossible to remember everything. I gave him a condensed version of what had been happening in his absence. He looked downright befuddled. Still, I did not mention my illogical choice to go hiking in the mountains alone, or the rescue of the puppy. I did, however, tell him about Whispers Bookstore and Vera's theory that perhaps these *things* were coming to me to help them with unfinished business.

"Can I see the letter?" Wally asked. "And what about the guy at the fountain? Did you find anything out about him?"

I shook my head, "To be honest, I don't think I told her about him. He really didn't interact, just stood there and stared at me. Yeah, sure, you can read the letter, it's in my room."

We drove back to the dorm and the first thing to greet us was the incessant barking and whining.

Wally placed a hand on my arm, "What in the hell is that?"

"Oh!" I said having totally forgotten about the puppy. A bad puppy mom, I'm telling you!

"That was another part of the adventures while you were gone."

"Red? Can I not leave you alone for twenty-four hours?" he teased.

We walked into my room and puppy ran to me happily peeing and jumping and squealing with delight. He didn't even glance at Wally. Finally, the puppy was satisfied he'd properly greeted me and ran to Wally. Wally bent down and ruffled his fur.

"Well, aren't you a cute little bugger," Wally said laughing as the puppy gnawed on his outstretched hand. "And what might your name be?"

I felt my face flush. I'd had the puppy for twenty-four hours and still hadn't named him!

"Ummm…well, you see, I, well, umm, I haven't gotten around to naming him yet," I said sheepishly.

"He's got some very interesting coloring," Wally observed, "his face is a little longer than most puppies."

"I have no idea what he's a mix of," I admitted. "I found him in the mountains. He apparently fell in the river and landed on some rocks. Poor thing was nearly starved and drowned."

"Uh, Red, I'll not pretend to be an expert, but I'm thinking you may have saved a wolf!" Wally said looking up at me in wonder.

Chapter Thirteen

"**A** wolf?" I repeated in disbelief.

"Yeah, I'm pretty sure that's what he is," Wally said nodding his head and still inspecting the puppy.

"Holy crap! What am I going to do with a wolf?" I cried.

"Can we take him back to the area you found him? Maybe his mom is looking for him," he suggested.

"Take him back?" I was surprised I felt tears in my eyes and my heart hurt.

"Well, Red, he is a wild animal even though he's cute and cuddly now. They have the potential to get huge and they have voracious appetites. How would you care for him? You can't keep him here in the dorm," Wally tried to reason with me. He was right of course. It was foolish of me to get so attached so quickly. I had no choice, really, but to take him back to the mountains and just hope for the best.

"Look, we have about a week and a half before school starts back up, maybe a week before some meandering staff starts to show up to get ready for the new semester. That's not much time. How about we take him back tomorrow?" he suggested.

"Tomorrow?" I nearly yelled. "I just got him! He might still be traumatized, or, or hungry!"

"Red," Wally said as though speaking to a child.

"No," I said simply. "I don't want to give him up. I'll find a temporary home for him until school is out, then I'll get an apartment or something, and keep him with me. I don't want to give him up, I *won't* give him up."

"Red, I understand, truly I do. I've had a dog in my life for most of my life, but, honey, this isn't a dog! It's a wolf!" Wally sounded as though I was trying his patience. "You can't just pick up a wild animal and decide to make it a pet. I'm not even sure you can legally keep one!"

I was getting angry now. I felt the rage rush through every vein, artery, and capillary.

"Don't call me honey, I'm not your honey. I should have never shown him to you," I sulked.

Wally sat on the bed and the puppy growled at him. We both looked at him in shock. His little hackles were up, his eyes focused on Wally. He growled again.

"Get up!" I shouted at him, "He doesn't want you sitting on the bed!"

Wally leaped to his feet and stood not certain what to do. The puppy put down his hackles and ran to get my shoe. He tussled and played with it, inviting us to join in.

"Holy, shit, Red. You have got to take him back!" Wally said with an urgency I'd never heard from him before.

"No. He stays with me. I'll hide him. I don't have a roommate and I have a week to ten days to teach him to behave. I don't know what I'll do but taking him back to the mountains is not an option. The conversation is over," I said stonily.

Wally shrugged. There really was nothing left to say on the subject.

Wally left without reading the letter. I felt very irritated with him. I sat on the floor and the puppy ran to me. In no time, I felt calmer and relaxed from the antics of my new charge. I wasn't sure how I was going to make this work, but I'd think of something.

Over the next week, we accomplished a lot. Wally kept his distance and to be honest, I really didn't miss him, or at least I didn't miss him enough to chase him down. He must have stayed in his room or down at the bar he liked to frequent. I had my hands full with potty training, how to use a puppy inside voice, and leaving my shoes alone. I was pretty sure people would notice the chewed-up leather, the missing heels, the rubber soles with bite marks, if anyone ever paid attention to me, which they didn't. I was also pretty sure I was going to have to come up with a name. Hey, You, just didn't cut it.

The day for puppy's final exam came when I realized I was out of dog food. He was growing very fast and Wally was right about one thing, his appetite was frightening! I explained to him that I needed to go into town and that he should be a good boy and lay down and take a nap.

"No barking, chewing, or peeing while I'm gone," I wagged my finger at him. "Don't bother anything, break anything, or chase anything. If you're a good boy, I'll see about giving you a proper name when I get home." He thumped his tail on the floor.

I waved at George as I sailed through the gate and busied myself with buying dog food, training treats, and as an impulse buy, a Kong, indestructible chew toy. I don't know about that, but we'll give it a try. I was a little nervous about leaving him at the dorm by himself, so I hurried back.

As I pulled in through the gate, I noticed George was not on duty. I pulled up the drive and into the parking lot. An unfamiliar van was in my parking space. I got my shopping bags and peeked at the side of the van. ANIMAL CONTROL,

Boulder, CO. gov I dropped the bags and raced to the dorm as fast as my legs could carry me.

I could hear talking, barking, and snarling as I took the steps two at a time. An arm shot out when I reached the top. Margaret stood angrily glaring at me. The animal control officer conferred with his partner.

"The safest thing to do is shoot him," the one said. The other nodded. "Someone is going to get hurt or worse if we try to just remove him."

"NO!" I screamed. I pushed Margaret so hard she fell against the wall. I didn't care, I hoped she would just continue falling down the stairs. I pushed past the two officers. They tried to grab my arms, but I burst through the door. The puppy was on guard at first and then when he realized it was me, he hung his head and put his tail between his legs. He thought he'd failed the test. He wouldn't get his new name after all.

I ran to him and fell to the floor gathering him in my arms. He whined. I buried my face in his fur and cried. As I sobbed, he lifted his muzzle and howled. He snuffled my neck and howled again.

The two officers had taken advantage of our moment and entered the room.

"Miss, we're going to have to take him now," one said softly.

"No! You can't!" I cried hysterically shaking my head.

"You can't have animals in a dorm," Margaret spat seething with anger.

"Then we'll go someplace. I'll take him back to the mountains. Please! Please, just don't hurt him!" I begged.

"Hey, Rog, let me talk to her," the officer who nodded at the suggestion of shooting my wolf, said as he stepped forward.

"You know it's illegal to have a wild animal for a pet, right?" he said softly.

I refused to acknowledge him.

"Unless you have a permit," he said.

I quit crying. I was listening. Muffled by the puppy's fur, I asked, "How do I get one of those?"

"If you will allow me to take him…"

My head shot up and I was ready to throat punch him.

"For now, just for now. I promise you I will personally look after him, 24/7 and I'll help you get the permit."

"You wanted to shoot him just a minute ago," I said suspiciously.

"No, I never said that. I said that would be the safest thing to do, and given the state he was in, I stand by my statement. Miss, I won't lie to you, I believe wild animals belong in the wild. That's their true nature, that's where their instincts serve them best. They were never meant to be cooped up in a small dorm room, but you and he have a bond, I can see that clear as day."

"You'll help? You promise you won't shoot him?" I was desperate.

"I promise," he said sincerely. Puppy licked his hand. That was proof enough for me.

I couldn't speak, only nod my head. I put puppy's head in my hands and made him look at me in the eyes.

"You need to go with this officer for now, not the other guy, he really would shoot you. But this one says he'll help us stay together, so be nice to him, okay? I will come to see you after class every day until we get this all sorted out. Do you understand me?"

The puppy wagged his tail and sat on his haunches looking up at the nice officer.

I had never, ever, in my entire life, felt as lonely as I did that night. Margaret wanted to put her two cents worth in. I closed the door in her face mid-sentence. She banged on the door a couple of times but then I heard her stomp off to her room. More than likely, taking her bottle of Vodka out from under the bed and washing away the taste of Probably Magic Sarangoski. I didn't have Vodka, so I cried myself to sleep.

I woke at some point during the night and saw Peter sitting beside the bed. At least I had one friend in the world. I closed my eyes and went back to sleep.

Chapter Fourteen

I woke feeling depressed and as the morning wore on, I started feeling angry. How did anyone know about the puppy? I had been so careful to keep him out of sight. I cleaned up after him. He pretty much stayed in my room, and though he was prone to barking and howling, on a campus this size and empty, the likelihood of hearing him anywhere was remote. The only person who knew the puppy was…Wally. Then I really got angry. I got seeing red angry.

He was getting back at me for the fight we had. He was staying away from me! That little worm had better stay under the rock he crawled under because I was going to use that rock to bash his ugly, little head in. I was seething. I began to feel like a warrior princess. Wally was the dragon terrorizing the sleepy little town and it was my mission to slay that dragon and present its head to the king! It had to be Wally!

I wanted to go into town and see my puppy. My heart ached and burned until I could put my nose in his fur, look into those puppy eyes and tell him how sorry I was that I couldn't keep him safe after all. I was so heartsick; I didn't even want to eat. I decided to go on into the Conservation headquarters and just sit and wait if need be until we could be together again.

The police station was gray brick and glass, full of odd sharp angles. Kind of modern, kind of strange. I walked in and saw the receptionist in a glassed-in office. I walked up and cleared my throat. The officer on duty looked up at me with a smug smile.

"Can I help you?"

"Yes. Animal control brought my dog in last night. I was told I could come visit him. I'd like to see him and make sure he's okay," I said politely.

The officer blinked at me, "We don't have visiting hours for dogs."

"No, you don't understand, see, I had, see, I go to school at the university and…um, well, I went hiking in the mountains and there was…it's complicated," I said because it really was! It really was very, very complicated.

"Name?" he asked.

"Oh, I never got around to naming him. I told him if he was a good boy when I got home from the store, he could have a treat and we would decide on a proper name," I explained.

The officer looked like he wanted to yawn. "*Your* name?"

"OH! Oh, gosh, I'm so sorry! Of course, my name is Probably Magic Sarangoski."

The officer started to write and then stopped, "It's what?"

"Probably Magic Sarangoski," I repeated.

I saw him start to write, he hesitated and looked at me suspiciously, "Can you spell that?"

"The whole thing?" I asked irritably. "You can't spell Probably Magic?"

"Miss, might I remind you, I'm sitting on this side of the desk, you're standing on that side of the desk. You walked in here and asked for my help. Not the other way around. Now, are you going to give me your name, your REAL name or not?"

I gave an exaggerated sigh and reached around for my backpack. He immediately stiffened and put his hand on his gun belt.

"Relax, Barney, keep the bullet in your pocket. I'm just going to get my driver's license to show you my real name," I'd had just about enough of these games. He held all the power and he knew it. I muttered under my breath, "Geez, another product of the public school."

I handed him my driver's license and you would have thought he was examining it to see if he should notify Homeland Security. I tapped my foot and fidgeted with the little pen on the chain at the window.

Disappointed I wasn't wanted by the FBI or something, he handed me my license.

"Satisfied?" I asked sarcastically.

"We get a lot of trouble from the college kids and their pranks. How the hell did you end up with a name like that?" he asked, shaking his head.

"It's complicated," I answered.

The door opened and the animal control officer from last night came in.

"Hey, Red!" he greeted me. "You here to see your friend?"

"Yeah. Is he okay? Did he do okay through the night? Did you feed him this morning? He's hungry all the time," I said talking so fast I was stumbling all over the words.

He smiled at me, "He's fine and most likely missing you as much as you're missing him. Bill, this is the lady with the wolf puppy. I'll take her back with me," he said to the officer behind the glass. I really, really wanted to stick my tongue out at Bill, but I restrained myself, and I was quite proud of that.

Puppy leaped against the cage bars when he saw me. I ran to him and put my arms through the bars and held on to him. He tried licking my face, but the bars were too close together.

I ruffled his fur and spoke to him as though he were a person, "Don't worry, baby, Wally is going to pay for this. I am so sorry I introduced you to him."

The officer wrinkled his brow, "Who is Wally?"

"The guy who turned us in," I said looking at him like I knew he knew that I knew that Wally knew.

"It wasn't a Wally who turned you in. It was the security guard, George," he informed me.

George? I thought we had a connection!

"Are you sure?"

He chuckled, "Oh, yeah, I'm sure. Seems our buddy George was running a drug business there on campus. He happened to see you out with the wolf, and he figured if we went after you it would distract us from him. He got fired and he's in a holding cell down the hall. Want to go see him?"

"Oh, my, gosh! George?" I said in disbelief. "And, umm, no, I don't want to go see him."

"By the way, my name is Aaron Jensen. Most people call me AJ. I was going to come see you today. I did some checking around with a friend of mine that works in Conservation and Wildlife Protection. She gave me a list of requirements, restrictions, you know, rules and regulations. I had her print them off for me. He's going to need some vaccinations and an exam. You have a vet you use?" he said helpfully.

"No, as a matter of fact, I've never owned a pet before. I don't even know where to start," I confessed feeling so very inadequate. Bad, dog mom. Bad, bad, mom.

"I think I can help you with that. You can file the permit with her as well, but, well, he's gonna have to have a name," he said slowly.

"He has one," I said. It came to me in a blinding flash of inspiration. I looked at my wolf puppy and smiled, "I knight thee, Sir Spirit Smoke!" I had my reasons.

Aaron laughed and told me it was odd, but appropriate, just like his owner.

"Can I take him home now?" I asked full of hope.

"Awwww…I'm afraid not until we get all the red tape untangled. If you'll come into my office, I'll get you started," he said helping me off the floor.

"Bye, Spirit!" I blew him a kiss and followed Aaron to his office. I could hear Spirit barking, trying to bring me back. George. I couldn't help it, it really stung. I never in my wildest dreams.

He threw a lot of information at me, a lot of papers to sign, appointments with the State Vet for the exam, shots, and neutering. I was exhausted by the time we finished.

"Will I get to take him back with me?" I asked feeling very accomplished.

Aaron laughed and shook his head, "'Fraid not. We'll keep him while all this is being done and I'll talk to the commissioner and see if we can count quarantine time concurrent with the time he's here for his processing. I'd say to plan on about two weeks."

"Two weeks!" I felt my heart thud against my chest.

"Yeah, but you can come down anytime you want and visit him. He'll be happy to see you," he tried to soothe me.

"You're right. I want to do this right. I don't want anyone ever again to be able to take him away."

Aaron cleared his throat and shuffled the papers, "Now, last order of business. The government doesn't do anything for free, so, how did you want to pay for this?"

I had not even considered how much it might cost! Oh boy, oh boy, what would I do if I had to go to mom and dad for the money?

"How much are we talking?" I asked while inwardly flinching.

"Hmmmm…okay, it says here $885.17," he said while checking the figures to make sure.

"No prob," I said bravely. How in the world was I going to come up with $885.17? I'd figure something out. I had two weeks.

I went back by Spirit's cage and told him about the meeting and promised him we'd be together soon. "Please behave for Aaron. He's our friend," I told him.

I was finally walking back to my car when I heard, "Hey, Red!"

Crap! I wasn't ready for this yet. Even though it turned out to be traitor George, I was still pretty miffed with Wally. I just continued to my car, got in, locked the doors, and backed out without even looking.

Chapter Fifteen

Wally accepted the slight, apparently. I didn't hear anything from him. I wasn't about to admit I missed him and his quirky ways, but Spirit missed him. I could tell. That's why when there was a knock on my door, I ran to get it...to ease Spirit's mourning. Spirit missed him. When I next visited my pup, I could tell him all was well, and Wally had apologized. Instead, there stood a glowering Margaret. She had a Band-Aid across her nose. Either she got schnockered and fell, or I hit my mark when I slammed the door in her face. Either way, it was a win-win for me. She practically threw an envelope at me and then quickly backed away. She never said a word.

I shut the door and sat on my bed looking at the envelope. It sure did look official, that can't be good. I was so exhausted, I didn't even care. Impulsively, I looked at Spirit's empty bed and said, "What do you say we blow this popsicle stand?"

I like to think we shared a special enough bond that he could pick up on my mood, no matter the distance between us.

I had to call mom and dad and discuss my change in plans. I knew just how to do it too. I went down to the Great Room. So, this is what it looks like! I wouldn't call it a Great Room, more like a Mediocre Room. It was in true Colorado

98

fashion with soaring ceilings and a stone fireplace. Seating groups invited mingling and socializing with other residents of the dorm. A hallway led off to the left, meeting with a flight of stairs. At the foot of the stairs was a kitchenette. I'd seen the kitchenette when I was foraging for leftover food after the girls left for Christmas Break. I had not ventured into the Mediocre Room. The sofas were done in forest green canvas and overstuffed armchairs in woodsy, lodge prints. Windows looked out over a campus lawn, dotted with Aspens, Oaks, and evergreens. It was a nice enough room, but it invited social interaction and that just ruined it.

Across the back wall were four privacy booths with telephones. I made my way into one of them and didn't even bother closing the door. Maybe Margaret would snoop and get an earful. At any rate, I took a deep breath and dialed my parent's number.

"Hello?" came my mother's voice over miles of telephone line.

"Hey, Mom," I said trying really hard to be enthusiastic.

"Probably! Oh, my dear! What a wonderful surprise! I have just been worried sick about you! How was your Christmas? Did you and your little friends have a Christmas Party?"

Good ol' Mom. Always one to hope for happy endings.

"Umm…yeah. It was good Mom, it really was. And you and Dad? How was your Christmas?" I regretted it as soon as I said it. Talk about opening a can of worms!

Mom's voice got sad, "Well, Sweetheart, when the very heart of your world, the breath we breathe, the reason our hearts beat, doesn't come home to celebrate, it's not much of a Christmas."

"I know, Mom, I'm sorry. I promise I'll make it up to you," I promised, not sure it was one I could keep or not.

"We did have quite the surprise though," she said cryptically.

"Oh?" I asked, intrigued.

"Yes. Christmas morning, Dad and I were just getting ready to sit down to breakfast when someone knocked on the door. You know, we kept some of the old traditions, even if you couldn't come home. We put an empty plate on the table while we ate our buckwheat pancakes with blueberries and rosehips. Oh! You'll never guess what your dad got me! He got me one of those juicy-blendy apparatuses and now we make...Ward! What are those things called we use that new thing for?" she yelled into the house.

I heard a distant, "Smoothies!"

She came back on the line, "Smoothies! That's what they're called. It's a new way we eat Kale and Strawberries and Bananas..."

"Mom, who was at the door?" I interrupted her to get her back on track.

"What? Oh, no one, dear, that was your dad telling me we now make smoothies," she said annoyed to be interrupted.

"No, Mom. On Christmas morning? Who knocked on your door?" I said, getting impatient.

"OH! I plum forgot what we were talking about. I got so excited about my Christmas gift," she laughed. "It really is the greatest..."

"Mom, I need you to focus. I have a better idea. Put Dad on the phone so I can say hi to him," I suggested, hoping she'd drop back into Earth's orbit by the time I finished talking to my dad.

"Ward! Guess who's on the phone?" she yelled.

I heard, "Probably. I heard you answer the phone."

"Well, she wants to say hi," my mom sang happily.

"Why? She can't come home for a sacred holiday, yet I'm supposed to run to the phone because she found time in her busy schedule…"

"Ward, be nice. You don't want her to stay away forever, do you? Don't be cranky," my mother stage whispered.

There was the usual clunking and static as the phone passed hands and I heard an audible sigh.

"Hey, there wayward daughter!" he said cheerfully. Did they not realize I could hear everything?

"Hey, Daddy. Again. I'm really sorry about Christmas. Sounds like you did have some excitement though. Mom said you guys had a visitor. Who was it?" I quickly got to the subject at hand.

"What? Oh, yeah. Aunt Jo. She's crazier than bat shit, but at least she found it in her heart to visit us," he whined.

"Aunt Jo?" I repeated in disbelief.

"Yeah, here's your mom," he said as the clunking and passing of hands was treated to a repeat performance.

"Hello, dear," my mom said once again. "Don't pay any attention to him. He's just upset because they took his favorite show off the air. He just hasn't dealt with it yet."

"Might try giving him some of your special cookies," I said snidely.

"You know, maybe I will! What a wonderful idea, Probably!"

"Okay, right. Mom? What did Aunt Jo want? Kind of weird for her to show up out of nowhere, isn't it?"

101

"Oh! Well, she wanted to talk to YOU!" she said as though that was about the silliest, craziest thing she'd ever heard.

"Me?" I gasped. "What about?"

"I have no idea. But she's weird like that, you know. Poor dear, the family hasn't heard from her in years!"

"Mom, I have to go now. They're getting ready for a student meeting to kick off the new semester," I lied. I just wanted to get off the phone. Shock? Dread? Why would my crazy Aunt Jo want to talk to me? As I was about to hang up, I suddenly remembered why I called in the first place.

"MOM!" I shouted into the phone.

"What, Probably?" she said clearly thinking she was going to finally end this awkward conversation.

"Mom, I've decided to drop out of school," I said simply.

There was a deafening silence.

"Mom?"

"I thought you were doing so well!" she said near tears.

"Oh, I am! But it suddenly occurred to me, I have always been 'doing something'. I've never really just been me. You know what it was like in school for me," I said quickly.

There was a snort on the other end of the line, "I still can't believe they let you graduate."

That stung, I'll admit that stung coming from my own mother. I hoped she helped herself to some of her special cookies.

"Yeah, me too. The thing is, Mom, I want to find out who I am. What my place is in this world. I'm going to classes and yet I have no idea what I want to be when I grow up. So, essentially, I'm going to school and I don't know why!" Though there was a grain of truth to what I was saying, it was my true agenda that really mattered and that my parents would never understand.

Again, silence. I heard her stage whisper again, "Ward! Come here. We have a crisis!" Much whispering back and forth. A couple of times the tone increased, then muffled again. Aha! She did know how to cover the phone for privacy. I tapped my foot and counted the knotholes in the booth.

Finally, "Probably, we understand how important it is to find yourself. You are right. You've never really been given a chance to explore who you are. Who you *really* are. Will you be coming back home?"

"Actually, I'd like to stay here in Colorado. I hike up in the mountains and I find it easy to think clearly up there," I said.

"Hike in the mountains? Alone?" she screeched. The most honest emotion I'd ever heard from my mom.

"It's okay, Mom. Really it is," I assured her.

"So, what? You're going to live up in the mountains like Grizzly Adams?" she asked.

Dad chimed in, "What? She's going to live in the mountains like Grizzly Adams?"

"Ward, please, I'm trying to find out," my mom said impatiently.

"Mom, no. I'm not going to live in the mountains. I just like to spend time up there. I'll get an apartment here. Maybe travel some. Soak in history, other cultures, you know, me, myself, and I."

An audible sigh of relief, "Well, that sounds nice, Probably. Much better than living in the wilds. You'd never get the sticks and leaves out of your hair!"

103

"Okay, the thing is, Mom, I don't have a job...yet. I might need some help...financially," I tried very hard to not sound like I was begging.

"Probably, this is something your father and I will have to discuss. I can't just give you an answer over the phone lickety-split. This is a huge undertaking with indefinite bounds...wait."

Whisper, whisper, you sure?

"Your dad says do it," she said, but I could hear the disapproval in her voice. It never occurred to me that maybe my parents didn't want me to come home as much as I didn't want to go home. Was this some kind of payoff? Still, the relief made my knees weak.

"I love you guys," I said, and I really meant it.

"We love you too, Probably. Keep us posted. At least send us your new address so we'll know where to send the money," she snapped. I could only hope they would heal. I was exhausted after that ballet of duck-and-dodge word war.

I hung up the phone and just sat there trying to gather my senses. That's when I looked up and saw Wally in the window waving a manila envelope. I stomped to the front door, flinging it open with my arms across my chest and one hip jutted out.

"What?" I growled.

Wally looked like he was about to reconsider but bravely pushed on, "Look. I know you're mad at me and I have to admit, I'm not entirely clear as to why, but I got to thinking about what you said. You know, about that ghost guy. I just kept thinking about it and decided to find out what I could about him. I typed and printed the report for you," he said quickly handing the envelope to me. "If you're interested," he added.

I snatched the envelope from him and gave him my most evil glare. "First off, I thought you wanted to be my friend. You didn't try to help me with Spirit, you just wanted to get rid of him."

"Who's Spirit?" he asked puzzled.

"MY puppy, you idiot," I snapped.

"Red, come on. Surely, even you can understand what taking in a wild animal can do! I was just trying to help in the only way I knew how. We're at school, you live in a dorm that doesn't allow pets, there are laws about owning wildlife, the list goes on. I was just trying to be reasonable because you weren't," he said defensively.

You know what? He was right. I wasn't being reasonable that night. In fact, I didn't even know it was a freakin' wolf! I wasn't quite ready to give up the fight, but the wind had definitely left my sails.

"So, you expect me to decipher all this by myself?" I countered.

I saw a smile creep to his face, and he said he would help me. If that was okay. I accepted.

We decided to meet in the cafeteria. I went upstairs and got my coat and gloves. When I got to the cafeteria, Wally sat with his faithful laptop open. I plopped down.

"Okay. I guess I need to update you on a few things. First of all, Spirit is with Animal Control..."

Wally's face blanched white and his eyes flashed blue sparks.

"Relax, it's okay. He's with an animal control officer who is helping us get him certified and legalfied and any other kind of –fied we might need. I should have him back with me in the next week." Wally visibly relaxed. "Secondly, someone turned us in, which is why animal control got involved. I thought it was you. That's the real reason I was so mad at you," I continued.

"Red! I would never, never in a hundred million years do something so hurtful to you! I'm a little hurt you would even think I would!" he exclaimed.

"Old news. I'll give you a benefit of a doubt next time. Turns out it was George the security guard, to hide the fact he was selling drugs from the gatehouse," I said dismissing his protest. "Anyway, Spirit is going through the routine and then he'll be home with me. That brings me to the final point. I'm dropping out of school."

He spat his drink and yelled, "What?"

"Yeah, I've already talked to my parents and they're going to support me while I look for a job and an apartment, which I'm thinking is a good thing. Mistress of Doom delivered a letter today from Dean Ragsdale. We have a meeting on Thursday morning, so I have two days to find somewhere to live," I finished finally taking a breath.

"Geez, Red, you wear me out," he said shaking his head. "I might be able to help though."

"I'm not taking money from you, Wally. I won't be beholden to anyone," I said stonily.

"How about Peter Euclid?" he said smugly.

"I don't understand," I said.

"It's in that paperwork. Seems our lovesick soldier did NOT die on Cemetery Ridge after all. Instead, he went back home, but Rosa was gone. He spent a couple of years looking for her, but couldn't find her. Finally, he went to work for the railway. In 1869 the first transcontinental railway was completed, and he got in on the ground floor. He worked in the final stages and then worked with the company until his death in 1899. He didn't trust banks, didn't have family to leave his money to, so he buried it somewhere. No one has been able to find it."

"I'm actually speechless," I said under my breath. "Do you think it's not so much the letter he wants delivered and more that he wants us to find his buried treasure?"

Wally's eyes brightened, "Us? Are you finally going to let me join you on this?"

"Did I say 'us'? I meant me. Awww...damnit, Wally, of course, I want you with me. I'm just really flabbergasted."

I felt my eyes drawn to the fountain. There stood that guy. Wally turned around and looked. "He back?"

I nodded. "And I got a bad feeling about this Wallace."

Chapter Sixteen

Wally, of course, didn't see him. It was then that he made a decision that would change both our lives. He stood up and sauntered to the fountain. I watched the guy watching Wally approach. I think I was curious as to whether the apparition would just disappear, or show himself to Wally, if they could even control just how visible they were and to whom. I really didn't know what would happen. I was curious and apprehensive.

Wally looked over at me and smiled. He pointed just left of the apparition and I shook my head. He jerked his head beside him and I nodded. The guy wasn't looking directly at Wally, more of a blank gaze, I guess I'd describe it.

Wally raised himself to look taller and puffed out his chest, looking all the world like a warrior Winnie-The-Pooh. I could tell he wasn't taking this seriously, my gut told me that might be a huge mistake. I don't know why I felt that way, I just did.

"Okay, Mr. Ghost Guy, you're upsetting the lady. It's time for you to go. You've had your fun, now hit the road," he said loudly.

The guy turned his head and stared at Wally. He slowly raised his arm and with palm exposed, Wally flew through the air! He crashed hard into the tables and chairs across the room.

I did the unthinkable: I screamed like a little girl! My heart missed a couple of beats, knocking the air out of me. The apparition disappeared. I must have teleported because I sure don't remember running across the room, but the next thing I knew I was bending over Wally. He must have hit his head on the edge of a table. Blood oozed across the floor beneath his head. He was out cold.

I didn't know what to do, so I began shaking him and slapping him in the face.

"Wally? Oh, God, Wally, wake up!" I heard someone screaming his name over and over, then I realized it was me. He finally began to rouse.

"Owwww!" he raised his hand to his head, and I caught it just in time. "What the hell just happened, Red?"

"We'll talk about it later. I need to get you back to the room. Your head is cut and it's bleeding pretty bad. Should I take you to the emergency room? I really think you're going to need stitches," I said, my voice shaking uncontrollably.

"Damn! That's gonna leave a mark," he mumbled and then passed out again.

I ran into the cafeteria kitchen and found a wall phone. I called 9-1-1 and somehow managed to get them the needed information. I kept looking around me to see if that bastard was hanging around. He was gone. I should have felt relief, but I worried when he might show up next and what he would do.

The ambulance arrived, along with Margaret and Dean Ragsdale. They were all talking at once. My head felt like it was going to explode, and I just wanted everyone to stop talking so I could think! The medics put pressure on the wound and bandaged him, then loaded him on a gurney and put him in the ambulance. With lights and sirens, they sped off the campus grounds. I just stood there looking at the puddle of blood on the floor. That was Wally's blood. Wally could have been killed! I realized someone was saying my name over and over. Dazed, I looked up and saw the angry faces of Dean and Margaret.

"Would you care to explain what happened here?" Dean demanded.

"I told you, you should have escorted her off the property when she assaulted *me*!" Margaret yelled hysterically. "Now, she's assaulted a *student*! How much more hell does she have to create before something is done with her?"

In unison, Dean and I both turned to her and said, "Would you just *shut up*?"

Margaret closed her mouth, but her anger was making her vibrate like a chainsaw.

Dean turned back to me. "What happened, Miss Sara—oh, hell, Probably what happened?"

I was still in shock. I still saw Wally flying through the air. I saw the blank look on that guy's dead face. Who would believe me?

I shook my head, "I honestly don't know."

Dean stood for a couple of moments not saying a word. Then, "We need to talk. Go to your room and pack, Probably, and meet me in my office in an hour."

"There's no need to talk, Dean Ragsdale. I'll be out by this evening. My parents are already aware. Right this minute though, I need to go to the hospital. I'm sure you understand. I have to make sure he's okay." With that, I turned and walked out of the cafeteria on legs with all the strength and fortitude of cooked noodles. I left them standing there wondering what in the hell happened and how were they going to handle the lawsuits sure to follow, and they didn't even want to think about the hit their institution would take once it hit the media.

I drove to the hospital and my mind was numb. I kept going over and over each and every second as though each one was a freeze-frame. I tried to remember what the guy looked like and then it hit me. My car slipped off the pavement and I heard the lane alerts thrum in protest. I jerked the car back on the road and pulled over in a safe spot. I had a strong, very strong idea, who that guy was. I think it was Rocco. He was a bully when he was alive, and he's a bully when he's dead. But what did he want? If he had any thoughts whatsoever that I was going to help him with any unfinished business, then he best be thinking again. I'd kill him if he wasn't already dead.

I began to calm down, so I finished my journey to the hospital. By the time I arrived, Wally was sporting thirteen new stitches and quite the impressive white bandage around his head. He laughed when I walked into his room.

"Hey, Red!" he chortled. "Look! I'm a Nigerian Prince and you, young lady, have won the Nigerian Lottery and I'm gonna send you millions and millions of dollars! For a small fee, of course, once it gets released, you know."

"Okay, so the pain meds are working," I said sarcastically.

"Yeah! It doesn't hurt at all!" he laughed.

"How long you gonna be here?" I foolishly asked.

"They're keeping him overnight, miss," I heard a voice enter the room. A bit on the jumpy side, I whirled around to see a nurse whoosh into the room.

"How are we doing, Mr. Jenkins?" she cooed.

Jenkins? Why didn't I know his last name was Jenkins? I'm not only a bad dog mom but I'm a rotten friend as well.

"I'm doing great!" he crowed.

The nurse smiled, "I know you are. Mr. Jenkins, I need to take your blood pressure and things. I need you to be very quiet for just a moment, okay?"

Wally put his finger to his lips and loudly said, "Shhhhhhhh..."

After she finished, she patted his arm. "Next time, try flying in an airplane with a pilot who knows how to operate a plane, okay?"

"Flying?" I asked when she'd left the room.

"I don't know why she said that," he said, looking just as confused.

"Since you're not dying or nothin', I need to get going," I said getting closer to the bed.

"Red? Don't go, okay?" he pleaded. "Please, stay here with me tonight."

I thought about needing to pack and be moved out by tomorrow morning. I would just live in my car, but it was way too cold out. It wasn't worth freezing to death over, Dean would simply have to adjust. I needn't have worried though, Wally was fast asleep with a goofy grin on his face. He reached out and took my hand. Without opening his eyes, he raised it to his lips and kissed it. I leaned down and kissed his forehead. Okay, the rest of the world was just going to have to back off for a few hours. I pulled up a chair and sat with my friend, all night long.

The next morning, I woke to skies that were gray and heavy. I could see the wind whipping the limbs on trees and stray street paper cartwheeling down the road. A plastic grocery bag filled with air and danced up to Wally's third-floor hospital room. My mouth felt full of sand and I was pretty sure my breath would peel paint. My back hurt, my legs hurt, my head hurt, I felt really yucky and dirty and grimy. Wally was still asleep. The nurse came in and I told her I was going to run down to the cafeteria and get some coffee. She nodded and continued checking Wally's vitals.

I thought about calling Dean Ragsdale, but I didn't have a damned cellphone. I really needed to bite the bullet and buy one! My steps felt sluggish and as I stepped onto the elevator, I leaned my head against the cool sheet metal wall. The air in my lungs felt old and stale, so I took as deep a breath as I could. The elevator dinged for the second floor and the doors slid open. There was a crowd of people staring into the car and I knew it was the dead seeking me out. I hit the close button and it snapped shut in their faces. I lay my head back against the wall and closed my eyes again.

I shuffled to the cafeteria, purchased a cup of coffee and a chocolate chip muffin. I sat at the table and chewed on autopilot. I was worried about Wally. I wondered again why Rocco felt the need for such violence and why was he stalking me? I worried about finding a place to live and finding a place to live that would let me have Spirit. I worried about…my head jerked up. A string of chocolate chip drool hung from my mouth and crumbs of muffin stuck to my forehead. It was going to be one long assed day.

Chapter Seventeen

Wally was being discharged. I offered to take him home, but he said his parents were coming up to take him back home for a few days. I hoped they weren't going to go into the dean's office and demand justice. This is where I had to have faith and not jump to conclusions like I did with Spirit being hauled off to jail. Though I was tired and depressed, I was only a couple of blocks away from Animal Control. I swung the car around to go visit Spirit.

When I walked in Aaron was at the front desk. "You look like hell," he greeted me.

"It's been a long night," I replied.

"Tell me about it," he sighed. "That wolf of yours got positively wild last night."

"What do you mean?" I asked, suddenly on alert.

"Oh, around 6:00 last night, he started running circles around the kennel. I tried to soothe him, and he bared his teeth at me. I got to admit, I was pretty scared of him at that point," Aaron explained. "Then he sat right in the middle of the floor and started howling. The most God-awful sound you ever heard. The hair on my arms stood up, it was so eerie. I decided right then, I was going to have to tranquilize him."

"Oh, no! You drugged him?" I panicked.

"Well, I was going to, but then I got to thinking how out of character that was for him. Something had to be wrong. So, instead, I went and sat by the cage and talked to him. I asked him if something was wrong. More howling. I asked if something was wrong with Red. He stopped and looked at me. I sat real still, then, amazingly, he walked over to me and hung his head and whined. At the risk of sounding like a crazy person, I called the university and asked if you were okay. They aren't real friendly over there, are they?"

"You don't know the half of it," I replied flatly.

"Anyway, I asked if you were okay and they told me there had been an accident involving one of the students, but it wasn't you. They were ready to hang up at that point. Red, that wolf knew you were in trouble of some kind. Weirdest thing I ever saw," he said shaking his head.

Not half as weird as the things I've been seeing, I thought to myself.

"Can I see him?" I asked.

"By all means! I was just getting ready to call you to ask you to come down so he'd know you were okay, but I couldn't find a number for you. I probably should have your cell number in case something else happens," he suggested.

"I…um…see? I don't have a cell phone," I confessed.

"You really should get one. You never know when you're gonna need one," he said as he stood to take me back to Spirit.

Spirit stood and raced to the edge of the kennel. I stuck my hand through the bars and ruffled his neck fur. Aaron surprised me by opening the kennel door. Spirit joyously leaped out of the kennel and into my arms. He was growing so fast! He was about mid-shin in just two weeks! There was no doubt in my mind that Aaron was taking very good care of him. I was grateful for that, but I'm unaccustomed to showing gratitude, so I just kept it to myself. Spirit finally calmed down and we sat on the floor together. I buried my face in his fur and cried. Aaron looked positively miserable and I wondered if he felt bad Spirit and I had to be separated.

"Hey, when you guys are finished, you mind putting him back in his kennel?" Aaron said with a husky tone.

"No, I don't mind at all," I said and kept my face hidden in that thick, lush fur.

I hated it, but I really needed to go face the firing squad. I needed to look at living quarters and I had a sneaking suspicion I was going to end up at Whispers Bookstore.

I drove slowly back to campus. There were dozens of cars going in and out of the entrance, as students returned from break and parents deposited said children back where they could be someone else's headache.

The new guard stepped from the gatehouse and held up a hand for me to stop.

"Miss Sarangoski?" he asked

"According to my driver's license," I said, with a smile, be that good or bad, but I was trying to be pleasant.

He walked around the guardhouse and returned with a two-wheeler full of boxes. "You want these in your trunk?" he asked blandly.

"What are they?" I asked suspiciously.

"Your belongings. I was ordered to not let you on campus grounds. If you'll pop the trunk, I'd be happy to put them in for you."

I popped the trunk and he put them in for me. I didn't realize I'd accumulated that much "stuff". Now, I was officially homeless. He went back to the back of the guardhouse and came back with a second two-wheeler full of boxes. I opened the backseat door and he deposited them on the seat.

"Is there more?" I asked.

"Just a couple of duffle bags, miss," he said as he swung them into the passenger side front seat. "Good luck, miss," he said and went back to his perch and Solitaire game.

I backed up until I could get turned around but there were so many cars in the way, I just loopy-looed on the perfectly manicured campus lawn. I saw the guard shake his head, but he didn't run after me. Just glad to get rid of me, I'm sure.

I drove around town for a couple of hours with no luck. Apartments didn't allow pets, small houses were out of my budget, there just wasn't a place to call home. Discouraged, I parked the car and walked to Whispers Bookstore. I'm not sure why, except it seemed on the surface, Miss Vera got me. She didn't call me weird, but of course, she was the epitome of weird, she didn't judge me, or dismiss me. I wasn't sure I liked being so dependent on friends all of a sudden. My life sure had changed. I didn't know what to do with it. It was like unwrapping a mystery gift and walking around and around it, mumbling, "What is that thing? What. The. Hell. Is. That. Thing?"

Miss Vera was waiting on the porch for me. She had her sweater pulled tight across her ample bosom. She didn't have her trademark smile that made you think she was either going to serve you milk and cookies or cut your head off with a meat cleaver. Today, she looked worried and upset. I ran up on the porch and she gathered me in her arms.

"Oh, you poor, poor dear! Come in, please come in!"

I did the only sensible thing to do, I burst into tears. We walked into the house still holding on to one another. She led me to the kitchen where it was warm, smelled good, and comforting. She sat me down in a chair. Today's special was cherry pie. Fresh from the oven, made with fresh fruit and lots and lots of whipped cream. The real stuff, not the stuff that squirted out of a can. I realized I was famished and no sooner thought it than a bowl of beef vegetable soup was set in front of me.

"You want to talk about it?" she said with sympathy tinging her voice.

I swallowed a spoonful of soup and nodded. "It's been crazy, Miss Vera. I don't even know where to start."

"More troubles with the dead?" she asked.

I nodded and took a gulp of milk. "They took Spirit away from me." As though that was the most traumatic thing to happen in the past two weeks.

"Spirit?" she asked scrunching her button nose.

"Oh, Lord, save me! So much has happened!" I wailed. Miss Vera patted my hand and nudged the soup bowl a little closer.

I finished the soup and pie. I felt more relaxed than I had felt in weeks! I was warm inside and out. Miss Vera didn't push, but before long I had told her the whole sordid tale. When I finished, she cleared the table, brought me a cup of hot cocoa, and sat with a frown.

"I don't like this. I don't like this at all. You really think that was Rocco?

"I'm not sure since I've never seen pictures of him, but he had on a black leather jacket, white t-shirt, and skinny jeans. He just had the look of someone of that era. It may not have been, but it sure felt like it."

"He must be afraid that you'll try to find Chuck and the other boys, which, of course, means you must!"

118

"Miss Vera, I really have a lot on my plate right now. I think Rocco's secret is safe for the time being. I need to find Rosa's family, I promised Peter," I complained. "AND I need to find a place to live and get Spirit out of jail and find a job…that's just what I need to do immediately, not to mention our buddy, Rocco, nearly killing a friend of mine."

"That concerns me a great deal. These apparitions rarely have that kind of power. Sometimes it's all they can do just to make an appearance. If he has the power to cause harm, then you may be dealing with a whole new monster, Probably. Be very, very careful. You'll need a protector. Is there anyone in your family you can talk to?" Miss Vera asked worriedly.

"No. No one," I said shaking my head. "Why do I need a protector?"

Miss Vera refilled my cup but didn't answer me. "As for finding a place to live, well, I have a garden shed out in the back, you're welcome to. It isn't much, but it's yours if you want it. There's a nice big fenced in yard for Spirit to get rid of energy and you're close to town. You could always look for someplace else as things settle down."

My first thought was: *Here it comes. Being held prisoner in a garden shed! Chained and denied sunlight and food until she tires of me!* Then I thought of Spirit and I was pretty sure he wouldn't let anyone hurt me. I decided to take a look at it anyway. What choice did I have?

We crunched through the snow in the backyard to a cute little cottage. Probably not more than eight hundred square feet. The porch was a tiny replica of Miss Vera's front porch with an arched trellis leading to the front door. It was yellow sided and trimmed in white. It looked sunny, in spite of the gray, heavy skies and threat of more snow.

Inside was like a fairy tale cottage. Bright curtains hung at the windows; the walls were ivory with slate blue trim. The kitchen had all the comforts of home except on a scaled down size. The bathroom had a shower, no tub, a sink, and a toilet. That's all I really needed. The bedroom had an oak dresser with plenty of room, a closet and a bed large enough to accommodate my large, awkward body. It was perfect.

"You can change anything you like. I want you to make it yours. If you need anything, just let me know and we'll get it," she said looking around as though afraid I wouldn't like it.

"It's perfect!" I gushed. Then, to my utmost surprise, I leaned down and hugged her!

She graced me with that girlish giggle and seemed pleased that I was happy.

"The only thing is, Miss Vera, I don't have any money. I don't have a job yet, and I still have to come up with over $800 to get Spirit out of jail," I pointed out in full disclosure.

"That's okay, Probably. I'm not using this shed anyway, it's just sitting here empty. It will be nice to have you here. Let's not worry about rent. As far as a job, well, to be honest, you already have one. I know the pay is very low, one would say non-existent, but it is a responsibility you cannot shirk. Let me help. I have plenty of money and my goodness! Who am I going to spend it on if not you?" the old woman seemed caught up in the moment.

While every fiber in my body wanted to scream in protest of taking anything from anyone, I was in an impossible situation and really did not have a list of options at my choosing. I nodded in agreement with a promise to pay her when my parents sent me money.

She waved me off with *phffff...* and led me back to the bedroom. She opened the closet and brought out clean, crisp sheets, blankets that were thick and woolly, pillows that felt like clouds, and a dog bed. That kind of creeped me out. She must have seen the look on my face.

"I had an old dog, named Rubio. He didn't like going into the house. He preferred to stay out here, so I fixed him up to be very comfortable. I'm sure some of his old toys are in here too," she said as she disappeared inside the cavern.

She reappeared with a treasure trove of toys. Everything looked comfortably worn but in excellent condition. I wondered if wolves played with toys. It seemed so, unwild. She finally placed her hands on her hips and blew out a breath.

"Well, I think that's it. I'm sure you can explore the kitchen and bathroom and find whatever you need. I'll leave you to get settled in." She turned to leave then turned back to me.

"I'm so glad you're here, Probably."

"Me too," I smiled, "and thank you. You saved my life."

With that, she was gone, and I was alone in my new home. She called it a garden shed, but to me, it was a mansion, my mansion.

Chapter Eighteen

I woke feeling well-rested and full of energy. I cannot remember when I felt so good! I wondered if Peter would know I'd changed residence. Boy, would that freak out the next girl in my old dorm room! I had other, more pressing things on my agenda this morning though. I smelled something delicious filling the house. I stumbled into the kitchen and found a pot of coffee and hot cinnamon rolls. A little note that said, *Welcome to your new home. A little housewarming gift for you.* I smiled. I knew I would never, ever cook like Miss Vera, so I appreciated her thinking of me and sharing.

After enjoying the treats, two cups of coffee, and shamelessly licking the plate of any errant icing, I went into the bathroom. There was a tall thin closet right behind the door. I opened it and saw bath linens, soap, shampoo, everything a girl could need. I stood in front of the mirror and looked at my reflection. Aaron was right, I looked like hell. I scrubbed my face clean and in a mad moment, I took a pair of scissors from the drawer and closed my eyes. Before I could lose my nerve, I picked up my ponytail and cut it off. When I opened my eyes, my hair splayed out like an Afro on steroids. I immediately felt regret. Like it wasn't bad enough before!

Depressed and angry, the good mood properly deflated, I stepped into the shower. I washed my hair and my body. I scrubbed until my scalp and body turned rosy, then I stood under the hot spray. I envisioned all the events and heaviness of the past several weeks, sloughing off, trickling down my long legs, traveling over my feet and disappearing down the drain. I finally stepped out and wrapped in a large, fluffy towel. I did feel renewed, but now I needed some desperate 9-1-1 for my hair mistake.

I wiped the fog from the mirror and stared in disbelief. My hair lay in waves and curls softly around my face. It fell to just below my ears, highlighting my green eyes and high cheekbones. The dark circles under my eyes were gone and I had a healthy glow I didn't remember ever having. I ran a comb through my hair. I want you to take a moment and just think about that. *I ran a comb through my hair!* I checked the shampoo and conditioner to see what brand. I didn't recognize it, but I wrote it down so I could always have a supply.

I dressed in jeans and a sweater with a cami beneath. I hated wearing bras and refused to do so. Besides, I didn't have enough boob to warrant a bra. T-shirts, sweatshirts, and sweaters hid a multitude of sins, sans bra, being one of them. I put on my woolen socks and heavy fur-lined boots and crunched my way to Miss Vera's backdoor.

She threw open the door with her million-dollar smile and greeted me with a good morning and then stopped mid-sentence. "Your hair!"

Self-consciously I reached up and touched it. Maybe it didn't look as good as I thought.

"I love it!" she exclaimed and clapped her hands.

I could feel myself blush heavily. I'd never had anyone take so much genuine joy in me. It felt good, but I worried it would make me soft. I would need to keep my edge in this new life, especially if Rocco was going to be a problem.

We chatted for a few minutes over hot cocoa, and then I told her I had some things to do. She didn't beg me to stay. She simply handed me my coat and made me promise I'd be careful in the predicted snowstorm. I had gotten so warm and cozy, basking in the glow of happiness, the wind was a brutal reminder that winter still held Colorado in its icy grip. I shivered as I ran for my car. I had to clear ice from the windshield, and then sit while the defroster finished the job. I backed out and headed to Animal Control.

I stomped slush from my boots as I entered the now familiar office. I removed a set of keys pegged to the wall that Aaron kept out for me. I was practically singing as I went down the hallway to see my best friend. Usually, I could hear him whining with impatience as I approached but when I got to the kennel, it was…empty.

Fear grabbed my heart and threatened to strangle the life out of it. My chest hurt; my vision blurred. Where was he? Did something happen? Did my application get denied?

A side door opened, and Aaron and a woman walked out laughing, with Spirit between them. He looked positively giddy! Aaron looked up and noticed me. He propelled the woman toward me, and she held out her hand.

"This is Mary Quanko, the state vet who has been caring for Spirit," he introduced her.

I held out my hand dumbly. She reached for it and pumped it a couple of times.

"You have one special pup there!" she beamed. "I'm going to miss him!"

I looked at Aaron with raised eyebrows.

"You can take him home any time you're ready. Almost didn't recognize you. Nice hair. I like it," he said grinning from ear to ear.

"I can take him home? But I don't have any money yet," I said.

"Already taken care of. Paid in full," he said through his smile.

Doctor Mary handed me some papers, admonished me to keep them in a safe place, showed off Spirit's new collar and jangling tags to show his vaccinations. Spirit was prancing proudly. I reached down and scratched his ears.

"But how...who?" I tried to ask.

"Anonymous," Aaron said, and the subject was dropped.

I wasn't sure what the protocol was. It had been such an intense, emotional two weeks, I was at a loss now that the ordeal was over.

"Thank you," was the best I could do. I walked slowly to the door with Spirit still prancing by my side. We walked to the car and I opened the passenger door and he jumped right in, sitting tall in the seat, staring straight ahead, with his tongue hanging out and a wide, bright smile on his face.

I wasn't quite prepared for bringing him home right this second and still needed to stop by the store to pick up a few things to outfit my kitchen cupboards. I got out of the car and so did Spirit.

"You can't go into a grocery store, good boy. You need to stay out here," I said trying to coax him back into the car. He wasn't having any part of that. I finally gave up and he trotted happily next to me into the store.

Customers google-eyed us, but I kept my eyes straight ahead, intent on my shopping list. Finally, the manager approached us. Spirit sat on his haunches and glared at the young kid.

"You can't bring dogs in here," he said with all the authority an eighteen-year-old thinks they have.

"Oh, that's good! I can certainly understand that," I said and moved on to the spaghetti aisle. I didn't know how to cook much, but I could whip up a killer spaghetti dinner. Now, which aisle was the Chef-Boy-Ar-Dee on?

"Ma'am, you'll have to take your dog outside."

I turned and looked at him and then gave a little laugh, "Oh, I do understand your confusion. He isn't a dog. He's a wolf. A Great Grey Wolf to be exact."

A heavyset woman set her full basket down and practically ran for the door. Other customers peeked around the corners and others replaced what they held in their hands and headed to the front.

"Dog. Wolf. Doesn't matter. No animals," he persisted.

Spirit had a low growl in his throat.

"Ummm...you might want to rethink your attitude. I don't think he likes it," I whispered mysteriously.

Another growl escaped.

The manager/kid backed away. "Next time, leave him home!"

I laughed and shook my head. I finished my shopping, taking a little longer than necessary because, by the time I got up to the checkout, the store was pretty much empty.

A perky little girl leaned over the conveyor belt and looked at Spirit. She briefly chewed her bottom lip and then looked me in the eye. "Can he have a doggy treat?"

We put our purchases in the car and I ruffed his fur and rubbed his head. "I haven't lost my edge at all!" I laughed. Spirit was back to panting and grinning with his tongue hanging out. I wouldn't have been the least bit surprised if he raised his paw in a high-five.

I brought in my groceries and set them on the kitchen table. Spirit ran through the house inspecting every nook and cranny. He found the dog bed and drug it over next to the bed. He wasn't so interested in the toys. He had a full-time job following me from room to room and adoring me. I fixed a cup of instant hot cocoa, which tasted nothing like Miss Vera's, but it would do.

The afternoon passed quite pleasantly with Spirit and I wrestling and playing on the floor. I let him out in the fenced-in yard, and he went crazy playing in the snow. I picked up snowballs and lobbed them at him. He tried to catch them, but they fell apart in his mighty jaws. We enjoyed some dinner and built a fire in the fireplace. The little house was heated by a wood stove located in the kitchen. The house must have been well insulated as in no time at all, it was warm and inviting. I loved my mansion and still marveled at the good fortune to have made friends with such a kind and generous woman.

All of a sudden, I wanted to talk to Wally. I wanted to show him my new home and share Spirit with him. I didn't have a cell phone though. I really needed to buy one. That was going to be my number one priority. Miss Vera visited to welcome Spirit home. She had baked peanut butter doggy treats. Spirit ate one and just like that, he and Miss Vera were BFFs. In fact, he was really taken with her. I felt an unjustified pang of jealousy, another new experience for me. I suspected all those carefully constructed walls were beginning to crumble. I wasn't sure how I felt about that.

Night finally made its appearance and as I closed the door behind Miss Vera, I realized I was exhausted. I hadn't made my bed that morning, and wished I had. The sheets would be cold. I changed into my pajamas, checked the mirror to make sure my hair wasn't standing on end as usual, brushed my teeth and washed my face. Spirit sat watching me with interest. I couldn't believe how happy I felt. I had friends. I had my own home. I had a companion. A feeling of forgiveness washed over me, even for Dean Ragsdale, Margaret, and George. I pitied people who never experienced this level of happiness and contentment.

I turned off the bathroom light, checked doors to make sure they were locked, and shuffled into the bedroom. As I walked into the bedroom to turn the nightstand light on, Spirit whined. I looked at him and saw Peter standing by the door. Though I really wanted to crawl into my amazing bed, I greeted him.

He looked upset. "I know, I know, I haven't paid the letter much mind yet," I said sheepishly.

His eyes looked angry. That concerned me. What if he had the same power as Rocco?

"Don't you get all attitude on me, young man!" I said angrily. "You weren't entirely honest with me. You didn't tell me anything about a hidden treasure. Don't you think that might have been a little bit important?"

"He says the money isn't as important as finding Rosa," a child's voice said.

I jumped and wildly looked for the source. I checked the windows, they were locked. The doors were locked. How did someone get in here?

"Who's there?" I asked.

"Me," came the answer.

"Is that you, Peter? Are you talking to me now?"

"No, Peter doesn't talk to you yet," came the reply.

My heart was thudding in my chest like a jackhammer. "Show yourself to me right now, or I'm calling the police!" I threatened.

"You can't. You don't have a cell phone. You really should get one, you know. And by the way? I'm down here."

I looked down and saw Spirit looking up at me. I shook my head. I'm dreaming, right? I felt my body begin to buzz and vibrate. I backed up to my nightstand. "No. Uh-uh. Dogs and wolves don't talk. I'm not freakin' Dr. Doolittle."

"Well, I do. I am your Translator. They can communicate through me," Spirit said clear as day.

"Yeah? Why don't they just talk to me?" I asked, not believing I was carrying on an actual conversation with a wolf.

"Because you haven't evolved. Can we be done with this conversation? Yeah, yeah, wolf talks, dead people appear, I get it, but honestly, Probably, I would think you'd be used to this by now. Peter needs you to get that letter to Rosa. It's important," Spirit said lowering his head and looking up at me. His eyes meant business.

Peter was still standing by the door, but he didn't look quite so angry.

"Okay, okay, I promise I will start in earnest tomorrow morning to track down Rosa's family. Can you give me any hints at all as to where to start?"

Peter shrugged and shook his head. Spirit put his paw on my leg, "He says, just try."

With that, Peter was gone. I looked down at my wolf. My head hurt. A talking wolf?

"So, how long have you been able to talk?" I asked sounding thoroughly insane. Aunt Jo would be proud.

Spirit thumped his tail and gave a little "inside voice" bark.

"Uh-uh, your secret is out, you little scoundrel. You talk to me," I admonished him.

His answer was to run in circles and stretch out his front paws with his hiney sticking up in the air.

"You brat. Now you're all dog?"

He answered by jumping on the bed, seeking the sweet spot.

"No, you have your own bed," I said snapping my fingers for him to get down. He just looked at me as though to say, *No spekanzie human.* I began to wonder if I imagined him talking. Too tired to sort it all out, I crawled in bed trying to scooch him from the middle. At some point in the night, he rolled over and pushed me right off the bed! I woke up on the floor, wrapped in a blanket. At least he let me have a cover.

The next morning, I sat going through the contents of the envelope Wally had assembled for me. Mr. Euclid was quite an interesting character! I went on a genealogy site and typed in Rosa's name. I didn't have much to go on except her name and the address on the love letter. To my surprise, I got results.

It appeared Rosa had never married nor had children. She came from a large family, twelve brothers and sisters. It seemed she was smack in the middle being the sixth child born to Louis and Maria Hargate. However, she did have a sister who seemed to flourish in the baby department. I clicked on the button for more information. Almeda married John Purvis in 1865. He was killed in the Civil War leaving Almeda with six children to raise. Her sister, Rosa, lived with her to help her care for the children. In 1886, Almeda contracted yellow fever and perished. Now, it was up to Rosa to raise the children alone.

I went back to the family tree and clicked on the family limb about the children. Of the six, only three survived to their twenties. Two girls and a boy. They went on to marry, reproduce, and lived to ripe old ages. At least, what was considered old age at that time. My eye kept going back to one of the nieces, Rosemary Clementine. She had five children, four sons, and a daughter. Rosemary's daughter, Julia, married a man named Andrew Berrymore. They had three children, two daughters, and a son. Rosemary died in 1923 at the age of forty. Julia was born when Rosemary was only seventeen years-old, in 1900. Wow! Imagine being born right on the cusp of a brand new century! Julia and Andrew Berrymore had five children. Three sons and two daughters. Very little information was available from this point on, but there was enough to know that one of the daughters, Lydia, was still alive today and living in Alabama. At least, there was no recorded date of death.

I calculated how old Lydia would be today. Her date of birth was September 20, 1926. The current year was 2001, so that would make her... ummm...seventy-five years old! Perfectly doable! I was starting to feel excited now! I switched over to White Pages and began to search for Lydia Jackson. Well, crap. There were fifteen Lydia Jacksons. How could I track her down? I really needed to get a cell phone. I didn't have one in this moment though, so I recorded the names and dates and decided to pay a visit to the local library.

Spirit lay curled up at my feet. "You want to go to the library with me?"

In answer he trotted to the door. "Still not talking?" I asked. Admittedly, had he answered, I probably would have had a heart attack.

As I was getting my coat and gloves on, someone knocked on my door. As much as I loved Miss Vera, I was on a mission and anxious to use the momentum my search had given me.

I answered the door and a woman stood on the step. She was dressed oddly, but her eyes were grass green. She wore an aviator's hat, a fur coat, long skirt and heavy fur lined flat boots. Her hair was divided into two long braids which hung over her shoulders.

"Can I help you?" I asked her.

"Are you Probably Magic?" she asked.

"You came to visit me," I said, hoping my snarkiness would discourage a sales talk.

"Of course. I'm looking for my niece, Probably Magic Sarangoski. I'm Aunt Jo."

Chapter Nineteen

I stood in bug-eyed disbelief. She stomped her feet and blew on her hands to get warm. Coming out of my trance, I invited her in. I led her to the kitchen where it was warm and fragrant. I couldn't quit looking at her. I noticed she had beads throughout her braids. No makeup, but her green eyes were bright and alert. Here, in my kitchen, sat the woman of many family stories and rumors, which had grown to legendary proportions. Part of *my* family and most likely crazier than bat shit, as my father so colorfully described her.

"Surprised to see me?" she smiled.

"That is the understatement of the year, Aunt Jo!" I replied honestly.

She laughed and I immediately felt a bond with her. Maybe I was crazy after all.

"Mom and Dad said you dropped by on Christmas," I said, hoping to coax her into a real conversation.

"No choice. I debated it for some time but finally thought, *'may as well get it over with'*. Now, there is one weird couple," she said shaking her head. "No offense intended."

I couldn't help but laugh, "None taken, trust me."

"Well, stand up here and let me get a good look at you. I haven't seen you since you were two or three years old." I obeyed and stood rather awkwardly for her to inspect. I was expecting the auction to begin any moment.

"You certainly got tall, didn't you? You get that from your Uncle Frank," she murmured. "That hair is all yours though. How'd you end up with that? Doesn't matter, but it sure does make you stand out, like the height wasn't enough. You always been this skinny?"

I was beginning to feel grossly uncomfortable and sat back down.

"It wasn't easy growing up between the hair and the name," I admitted.

"I'd say not, but Probably, all things have a reason," she said nodding her head.

"How are you doing with the spooks?" she asked bluntly.

"Pardon?" I snapped.

"Oh, come on, are you seriously going to sit there and deny you're seeing spooks? Ghosts? Apparitions?"

"Yes! No. Maybe..." I was losing and I knew it. She looked down her nose at me.

"Okay, but I don't go around broadcasting it. People will think-" I cut it off mid-sentence.

"Crazy like your Aunt Jo?" she finished for me. "Probably, you can't go around caring what people think of you. You have to be true to yourself. No one knows your truth like you do. No one can live your life but you. If you always try to fit into their mold, you will never realize or reach your potential to just be you."

She was right, of course. I had lived my first nineteen years not caring what people thought, then I started making friends, giving life a chance, being willing to be vulnerable. Things had changed, but did that mean the core of me had to change as well? It suddenly made sense why my family made jokes and whispered in each other's ear about Aunt Jo. She didn't care what other people thought. She was just true to herself and people didn't understand so they shut her out.

"So, are you one of *those?*" I asked trying to be delicate.

"Yeah, I am. As a matter of fact, that's why I've been trying to track you down," she said as she settled more comfortably in her chair.

Spirit stood up from in front of the stove and lay his head in Aunt Jo's lap. "Well, hey there, big fella. How have you been?"

I cocked my head and asked out of curiosity, "You act like you know him."

Aunt Jo gave Spirit an affectionate head pet, "Oh, he's been around a very long time. He's been a Champ, a King, a Rubio-"

"Rubio?" I swear this woman was going to give me a heart attack. Rubio was the dog Miss Vera had!

"Sure! He gets his assignments too!" Aunt Jo exclaimed.

"Assignments?" I didn't understand this conversation at all, and it was giving me a headache.

Aunt Jo cocked her head at me and looked down her nose, "Are you hard of hearing or just not paying attention?"

"Aunt Jo, all this is overwhelming. I don't know what to believe anymore. I'm afraid to trust what I see, who I meet, what happens...I just don't understand!" Frustration was bubbling up from my toes and I felt like I was going to implode. They would find me tucked into a corner, rolled into a little ball, eating lime Jell-O.

Aunt Jo sighed heavily, "Okay. You got any coffee in this place? It's going to be a long night, Probably. I wish we could ease into this, but you're in danger and I just don't have the time to hold your hand."

Feeling a little stung by her sharpness, I dutifully went to the coffee maker and put on a pot of coffee. I set out lemon iced sugar cookies and fresh blueberries. Once it brewed, I poured up two cups and sat back down.

"Okay, I'm ready now," not at all sure I was ready.

"I realized I had something special about me when I was just a child," she began. "Things would happen, and I would have certain 'feelings' if you will. By the time I was a teenager, I discovered that my presence could change these things. I happened upon an old antique shop called Whispers Antiques and Collectibles. There was an old woman who ran it, named Vera Johnson."

"You mean MY Vera?" I interrupted.

"Most likely. I haven't met YOUR Vera, but I'd say so. I noticed a sign out front that said Whispers Bookstore and since I don't believe in coincidences, I'd say the probability is high. Did you feel drawn into the bookstore?"

I nodded.

"Did she seem to know things about you?"

Again, I nodded.

"Did you just happen to need a place to stay?"

I felt my breathing become shallow and my head swim.

"She's a witch?" I breathed.

"Good lord, no!" my aunt laughed. "She's a Coordinator!"

"Anyway, to carry on with your crash course of all things unexplained and misunderstood...I began to receive assignments if you will. My first big assignment was back in 1976. The Vietnam War had just...well, let's be polite and say it had just ended. Those were tumultuous years. The country

137

was still deeply torn apart. An entire generation had spent its adolescence protesting, fighting the establishment, and burying its dead. There was one couple though, in my circle, that was so lost, they were losing themselves in the aftermath. They agreed that to drive home the need for peace, they would kill themselves, on the White House steps, right in front of the President of the United States. Oh, they were very serious. No amount of talking or reasoning would change their minds. They truly believed their public display of the ravages of war, would drive home the need for peace and unity."

"Oh, my gosh! That was pretty extreme!" I exclaimed as I imagined how passionate they must have been to go to such drastic lengths to make a point.

Aunt Jo nodded and continued, "Anyway, I got one of those *feelings,* that I needed to be close to them, so I traveled to Washington D.C. and waited for them. They arrived a short time later and I watched as they made their preparations. They had somehow procured a plant called Nightshade and made a cocktail with red food coloring, to represent the blood of the soldiers killed in a ridiculous skirmish. I had to act fast, because once that poison touched their lips, it would quickly kill them."

"What did you do?" I asked about to jump out of my skin.

"Well, I walked up to them and asked for directions to the Washington Monument!" Aunt Jo exclaimed as though that was the most sensible thing in the world to do.

I wasn't expecting that answer and reared back in my chair with confusion.

"I distracted them from their mission," she explained. "And while they were giving me the directions and carrying a very nice conversation, I removed the poisonous drink and replaced it with fruit juice. I don't have strong spell powers, but I can do certain small things. When I was satisfied, they would be okay, I simply left them standing there. I knew they would try again and again until they finally succeeded, so I protected them by putting their lives on a continuous hold. Harmless resentment against big government, unnecessary wars, advanced technology, just a bubble of time where they felt most useful and at inner peace. I could see the bubble was still well in place when I went there over Christmas."

"Mom and Dad?" I yelled.

Aunt Jo nodded, "Didn't you ever wonder about their weirdness? Their refusal to acknowledge the advancement of life around them?"

"Oh, I more than wondered," I admitted, but suddenly it all made sense. "But does that mean you're not *really* my aunt?"

"I'm a *Protector*," she said. "As far as your family is concerned, I'm part of the family. A distant relative of a relative of a relative. Kind of like a family friend that has gained family status. But, to answer your question, no, I'm not blood related to you."

"So, you're what? Like a guardian angel or something?"

Aunt Jo waved her hand at me and snorted, "Guardian Angels are something people made up, so they didn't have to face their loved ones were really gone. It's kind of like a comfort blankie. I'm the one who changes events to protect a person from an untimely death. Right now, I'm your Protector."

"I don't need a Protector," I said simply as I stood to refill our cups.

"Yes. You do," she quipped.

"No. I don't."

"You do."

"I don't."

"Probably, my assignments are never wrong. You need a Protector."

"Look, poor old Peter is harmless. He wants to tell the love of his life about his undying love for her. I hardly see any danger in that."

"You seem to think this is an isolated incident. It's not. You're in danger and I'm sworn to protect you on your quest."

"Well, Aunt Jo, you did a really crappy job of protection. My friend was nearly killed! Where was all that *super power* then?" I said hotly. I could feel anger starting to take hold.

Aunt Jo shook her head and then looked me straight in the eye, "Why do you suppose he *wasn't* killed? And how do you know but what the demon wasn't after you?"

She had me there. Not quite willing to admit defeat, I sat heavily in my chair and pouted. "I don't need a Protector."

"Well, you do, and you got one, so deal with it."

Chapter Twenty

We talked through the night. The sun was just beginning to lighten the sky when she abruptly stood and gathered her coat and aviator hat.

"You're going?" I asked.

"Well, yeah. I got other things to do other than sitting around here all the time," she snapped.

"How will you know I need help? How do I contact you?"

"You do your job and I'll do mine," she finished buttoning her coat and adjusted the ear flaps on her hat.

She opened the door, and then turned around, "Be careful, Probably, I can only do so much, and your stubbornness worries me. Bye, Spirit! Take care of our girl."

With that, she was crunching her way through the snow. I didn't see a car parked close by or a broom leaning against the house. I wondered if she walked everywhere or if she could fly. I felt like slapping myself in the face. This had to be the most bizarre night in the history of the world and most assuredly, in my life. Still, much of what she had said made sense.

I wished I had someone objective to talk to about all this. I needed to talk to level-headed Wally. I needed my one true, sane friend. I seemed to be attracting every crackpot in the 'outer realm' to my doorstep, even my furry companion was part of the conspiracy! I felt an overwhelming need to lie down, get lost in sleep, and recharge my sensibilities so I could sort it all out. I wanted to talk to Miss Vera, but even more, I wanted to be alone. I felt that my life was assaulting me from every direction.

I let Spirit play in the snow for a while, then called him in and said we were going to take a nap. Apparently, the Fickle Finger of Fate thought that was funny because just as I got ready to claim my sliver of a spot in bed, there was another knock on the door. Like a petulant child, I stomped to the door and threw it open. Then I just fell into waiting arms.

"Geez, Red, it would have been nice if you told me where you were living now!" Wally laughed.

I was so happy to see him! He didn't look the worse for wear. I invited him in and had him sit in my 'living room'. Spirit immediately jumped on his lap and smothered him with kisses.

"Yeah, yeah, I missed you too, you big goofball," he said ineffective in warding off the tongue.

"How are you feeling?" I asked.

"Great! Still getting some headaches now and again, but nothing I can't handle. This is a really nice place, Red!"

I blushed, "I think so too. I wish I could take credit, but I can't. Miss Vera was kind enough to offer and I was desperate enough to accept."

"So, let's talk," he said, getting Spirit settled at his feet.

"Okay. What about?" though I had a pretty good idea.

"I wish I could start the conversation, Red, but I don't know what the hell even happened."

"Yeah, about that...I'm really sorry," and I was too!

"No apology needed, just an explanation. Just so you know, I believe you 100% now. I just want to know what happened. Did it have to do with that guy you saw at the fountain?"

I nodded and tried to find a good starting point. "Well, I think he was trying to warn me off. I'm not sure what I'm supposed to be staying away from yet, but he definitely was sending a message. I think it was Rocco."

"And who's Rocco?" he asked.

"Remember the boys in the Cadillac?"

I could see the memory flash through his mind. I told him of what I'd learned about the horrible accident.

"Maybe he's afraid you'll find Chuck and his friends," he suggested.

Suddenly, like a white, blinding light, it all made sense! Wally just may have hit upon something! "Then we have no choice, we have to find that Cadillac!"

Wally didn't look so sure.

"We have a 'Protector' now, Wally. Things have gotten real serious since you've been away."

Wally rubbed his head, "I'd say it's already gotten serious."

Barely taking a breath, I told him all that had transpired over the past several days. His face showed a variety of emotions as I talked as fast as I could. Disbelief, belief, doubt, acceptance, understanding...it was like turning pages in a book with stop-frame pictures.

When I finished, I leaned toward him, "You have any questions?"

"Yeah," he said, nodding his head. He looked thoughtful and then cocked his head, "You got anything to eat?"

My Wally was back.

The rest of the afternoon we poured over Peter's history. I could not find a single clue as to how to track down

Rosa's family. I did have a lead on her great-great-great-niece, but hadn't the time to take it any further. With Wally back, I had reinforcements. He wanted to help as much as he could without taking time from his education.

"Did you ever get a cell phone?" he asked the dreaded question.

Sheepishly, I shook my head. I was really going to have to make that a priority. "But I will!"

"You've only been saying that for the past five months, Red," he chastised me.

"No! I'm serious. I really will," I said with full commitment.

"Uh-huh," he smiled.

I showed Wally my roughly drawn family tree for the Hargate Family. We decided to try to call the Lydia Jackson I found through White Pages. We went to Miss Vera's back door and asked if we could use her phone. She said yes, then discreetly left us to our task.

The phone rang in my ear. Part of me wanted it answered, and part of me desperately hoped no one was home. *Ring. Ring, Ring.* I was just getting ready to hang up when I heard a break in the rings.

"Hello?" said an older woman.

"Yes, ma'am, is this Mrs. Lydia Jackson?" I asked.

"You called me. Don't you know who you're calling?" came the raspy voice. I could hear just the slightest hint of an accent.

"Yes, ma'am," I said quickly. "I'm looking for a Lydia Jackson. Are you related to a Rosa Hargate?"

"Young lady, I'm not interested in anything you're sellin'. Got what I need and more than I want. Do not call me again."

"No! Wait! Please, Mrs. Jackson, I'm not selling anything! I have something that belongs to your family!" I shouted before she could hang up.

"What would that be?" she asked interested now.

"It's a letter. It was written during the Civil War to your great-great-great aunt. It's a love letter addressed to Rosa Hargate from Peter Euclid."

"Peter Euclid? Lord, I haven't heard that name since mama died," the old woman said softly.

"So, you know him?" I asked hoping against hope.

"Know him? No, I don't believe I do. I don't know how old you think I am, but I can assure you I'm not two hundred years old!"

Embarrassed by such a simple mistake, I picked my next words carefully. "Mrs. Jackson, I believe Rosa's family is meant to have this letter. I would like to deliver it to you. We can meet anywhere you like, with as many people with you as you like. I know I'd be suspicious if someone called me out of the blue like this. I promise you with every beat of my heart, I am sincere."

There was silence on the line. I was afraid she had hung up. Perhaps I had blown the only lead I had to carry out Peter's wishes.

"What is your name, young lady," she asked. I really, really didn't want to tell her. If I told her my name was Probably Magic, she would think for sure there was a crackpot calling her.

"Melissa King," I lied, "but my friends call me Red." That part was true, at any rate.

"That's not a very girly nickname," she huffed.

"It's okay. I'm not a very girly girl," popped out of my mouth before I realized the words had even occurred to me.

146

There was a throaty laugh and she said with a smile I could feel across the miles of phone line, "I like you. Okay, are you local?"

This part had not even crossed my mind, I was living in Colorado and she was in Alabama, several hours away.

"No, ma'am, I'm actually in Boulder, Colorado, but I will drive to Alabama if that's what it takes to get this letter to you," I confessed.

"It's been a long time since I've been on a road trip. Would you mind if I came to see you?" she suggested.

Taken aback, I felt my mouth opening and closing like a fish out of water, "No! That would be lovely! Are you sure? It's quite a long way."

"I used to be quite the thrill-seeker," she said with a youthful lilt in her voice. "If you don't mind, I would love the opportunity to have one last thrill."

We made plans for the second week in March, just a short one month away. Plenty of time to do more research and find out even more about my star-crossed lovers. We were about to have our first official investigation.

We hung up and I felt I had just scored. I, actually, was looking forward to Lydia Jackson's visit! I thanked Miss Vera for the use of her phone, and we went back to my cottage. As I neared the door, I saw a man in a long black coat knocking on my door, or at least, that's what it looked like.

"Can I help you?" I called to him.

He turned slowly. "Are you Probably Magic Sarangoski?"

"All depends on who wants to know," I quipped.

The man glared at us, then rushed off the porch, knocking me a little to the side, got into a black car, and left. Wally didn't have time to react to anything that was taking place. The whole thing couldn't have taken more than fifteen seconds. I had a bad feeling.

"Who was that?" Wally asked watching the black car speed away from the curb.

Spirit was jumping at the front window, making an unholy sound, he was desperate to get out. I shook my head and we went into my house. Spirit circled me sniffing furiously.

The ambience of the house had changed. It was cold and foreboding. It didn't feel safe anymore. That's when I saw it. Peter's letter lay on the floor, chairs were knocked over, and the box I kept my research in was emptied. My heart thudded heavily in my chest. My home, my safe haven, had been breached. What were they looking for? Peter's buried treasure?

I would call the police, but…I didn't have a cell phone. I really needed to get one. Especially now that my life had taken some troubling turns.

I picked up the papers and replaced them in the box, righted the chairs, and lovingly picked up Peter's letter. I was trying to find his one true love, could someone else be trying to find his money? Why didn't Spirit chase them away? What good was a guard wolf if he didn't guard?

Wally did not like leaving me alone. He fidgeted and hem-hawed that he should at least spend the night to make sure our stranger didn't make a late-night appearance. I shook my head and assured him I would be fine. I had fighting skills and Spirit was there as well. I made him go home with the promise we would talk more in the morning.

That night, before slipping into bed, I double-checked all the windows and doors to make sure they were securely locked. As added insurance, I put a baseball bat directly under the bed. They wouldn't catch me unawares again!

Peter visited and I filled him in on the progress I made. I decided to take a chance and mention the buried treasure. He looked alarmed. I looked at Spirit.

"Is he saying anything?" I asked my wolf.

"No, other than, that is not the most important thing. The letter. The letter must be delivered to Rosa," Spirit said sitting on his haunches.

"Well, even so, if people are going to be breaking into my home, going through my things, and perhaps cause me harm, I'd kinda like to know what I'm getting into!" I replied angrily.

"Forget the money," Spirit translated. "Besides, death isn't all that bad."

I looked straight at Peter, "Yeah? Well, you aren't exactly the poster child for death."

He disappeared. I was glad. I'd had about enough for one day.

Chapter Twenty-One

I woke up to a loud banging on my door. I looked at the clock beside my bed. 5:10 AM. Seriously? I stumbled out of bed and answered the door. Wally nearly fell into the house. He had some kind of a mad, glazed-over look on his face and was talking so loud and so fast, I could barely understand him.

I sat him at the kitchen table and put the tea kettle on. He was fidgeting and tapping his fingers. What on earth was wrong with him?

I placed a cup of tea in front of him. "What is going on?"

He looked at me and broke out into a grin. "I know what happened to Chuck! It's all related!"

"What are you talking about?" I asked, still not understanding.

"Peter, Chuck, Rocco, it's all related!" he repeated.

"I got that much. HOW, are they all related? You do know these events are two hundred years apart, right? Start at the beginning," I said putting some bread in the toaster. I was tempted to make cinnamon rolls, but given his frogginess, I was reluctant to feed him any sugar.

"Okay," he said taking a deep breath, "Last night, I stopped in at an antique store to just kinda look around."

"I didn't know you liked antiques," I said amazed at this new tidbit about my friend. Didn't know he had brothers and sisters, didn't know his last name was Jenkins, didn't know he likes antiques…what else didn't I know?

"I don't really. I mean, I don't dislike them, but I'm not like, some great antiquer or anything. I just went in because the stuff in the window looked interesting, so I thought I would give it a look-see. Ya know? You know how sometimes things just catch your eye? Well, I saw these old eyeglasses and they just really caught my attention. Maybe because I wear glasses. I've worn glasses for as long as I can remember. When I was about six…"

"Ahem…" I kind of coughed.

"What? Oh yeah, okay, so I went in and there was this really old guy behind the counter. I asked him about the eyeglasses," he went on with his tale.

"Wally, this is all very interesting, said no one ever, but what does it have to do with Peter, Chuck, and Rocco?" I asked getting impatient with the scenic route to the meat of the conversation that woke me up at 5:00 in the morning.

"I'm getting to that, Miss Impatient! He said the glasses were from the late 1800s. Said they were brought in by some lady who wanted to know if he would buy them from her. She said they belonged to a distant relative, get this, Peter Euclid!" Wally sat back in his chair and puffed out his chest with pride.

"I'll give you that," I conceded. "That is weird. Wonder if there's any connection to Lydia Jackson?"

"I bought them," he declared. "That's not all! While the old guy was getting the glasses out of the window display, I happened to look up and saw a framed newspaper clipping. It was about the accident of Chuck Doup!"

"NO!" I breathed. "But how do the two tie together?"

"Geez, Red, you going to let me tell the story or what?" he said exasperated.

I made a zipping gesture with my lips. "Shutting up," I said properly chastised.

"Okay, where was I?" he asked scrunching up his face.

"You saw the article," I prompted.

He looked at me with a smile, "I think your zipper is broken."

I smiled back, "Fixed it. I won't say another word until you tell me to."

"Okay, so I saw that article and I asked him about it. He took it off the wall and handed it to me. I asked him, 'Is it true they never found Chuck or his Cadillac?' He says that ain't the whole story. Turns out, he knew Chuck! He remembers that day like it was yesterday. So, I asked him what the whole story was. He proceeds to tell me that Chuck and his friends went to Charleston, South Carolina for a Cadillac rally. They thought it would be fun, except it wasn't. They got bored and decided to do some cave exploring. Well, to make a long story short, they found a big ol' chest way back in the back of one of those caves. Being kids, they, of course, had to drag it outside and open it. When they finally got it open, it was full of money!"

I could feel my eyes widen until I thought they would pop out. Was that Peter's treasure? Oh, how I wanted to ask the thousand questions banging around in my brain! Instead, I enthusiastically bounced around in my chair, waving my hand in the air like we did in second grade. Like my teacher, Wally ignored me too.

"Mr. Dempsy, that's the old guy's name, said the boys put the chest in the trunk of the car. They all had plans of how they'd spend this unexpected windfall, but Chuck was a good kid. He said they should take it to the police station and report it. They drove around all weekend with that money in the trunk of the Cadillac arguing about what they should do with it and never made it to the police station. Since there was some Confederate money in the bottom part, one of the boys, I think it was Ronald, Donald, something like that, suggested talking to the Heritage Society and see if maybe one of the historical museums would want to buy it. At any rate, Monday morning, when they got to school, they couldn't help but show it off to other kids. When they opened the chest a slip of paper fell out of the cracked liner in the lid. Mr. Dempsy said he picked it up and handed it to Chuck."

"I'll bet Rocco was one of the kids he showed the money to," I mused.

"Mr. Dempsy didn't specifically say, or it could be, Rocco just heard about it. I'm sure everyone was talking about it," Wally said. "By the way, you're rotten at keeping quiet. Anyway, the boys were laughing and horsing around, and Chuck read the note aloud.

The treasure therein belongs to the best

Woe to those who are so much less.

"That money was for Rosa!" I exclaimed. "That's why he wants to make sure Rosa gets the letter!"

"And Rocco showed up about the same time as Peter," Wally pointed out. "He's following Peter hoping he'll lead him to the money."

I thought about that. I never really thought about greed and underhanded dealings in the spirit world. Perhaps one's personality carried over to the other side? Why would Rocco want the money so badly? What could he do with it?

"There's more," Wally interrupted my thoughts. "Apparently, Rosa's family got wind of the money way back when. They've tried everything to find the money, hired treasure hunters, private investigators, mystery TV shows, but no one has ever found it."

"Well, wouldn't it go to Rosa's family anyway?" I asked, not exactly sure what it would mean to 'give it to Rosa'. She would have been dead for many years.

"I don't understand what I'm supposed to do!" I said more exasperated by the minute.

"I don't know, but we'd better figure it out before Rocco does," Wally warned.

"My head hurts," I said rubbing my forehead. Too much complicated thinking this early in the morning makes Red a cranky girl.

"I don't like it," Wally said shaking his head.

"I don't either, but I'm not sure what to do. More research I guess," I said with a heavy sigh.

"No, I mean, I don't like your new hairstyle," Wally said pointing to his own head of black enviable curls.

"What?" I felt like I was coming out of a trance and there had been a whole different conversation going on I was unaware of.

"Your hair. I mean, it looks really nice, but on someone else. You need your original style back."

"That frizzy, rat's nest?" I asked amazed he had even noticed.

"Yeah. That was you. Just as much a part of you as that stubborn attitude," he explained. "And why did you cut it? Now, you just look like any other 'girl'."

I was taken aback. I looked like any other girl? All those years of angst, of fighting with my hair, my name, my lack of feminity, desperately trying to look like all the other girls, and here was someone who actually liked all that? Truth be told, I kinda missed it too. I figured it was just because it was what I

154

was used to, but with the smooth, wavy hair, the new friends, the unexpected turn of my life, suddenly feeling like I finally found the groove of life, I had stepped out of my comfort zone and into the realm of my desire to be normal. Maybe that wasn't what I wanted after all. Maybe some small part of me, the voice in my soul I kept telling to shut up, actually liked who I was.

Spirit stood up and laid his head in my lap.

"You too?" I asked him as I scratched along his jawline.

Out of the corner of my eye, I sensed a movement. Peter? I stood and looked out the window. For the briefest of moments, almost like a fleeting shadow, I saw a figure dart out of the yard and behind the hedges. My heart skipped a beat. Was someone spying on me?

"You see something?" Wally looked up with a piece of toast halfway to his mouth.

I tried to envision what I thought I saw. It was just too brief to be sure. Could have been the shadows from the trees in the early morning dawn. I shook my head.

"I have a feeling, we find Chuck and the Cadillac, we'll find the answers to everything," I said as I sat back down.

"Hey, how about I take you to Waffle House for breakfast?" Wally invited. "All this detective work has me starving."

I was still strangely troubled by the shadow. Little did I know, Rocco wasn't the only one keeping tabs on me.

"Me too," I agreed, "besides, I'd like to talk to this Dempsy guy."

We finished a breakfast that earned the waitress a great tip. With bellies full, we started to walk to the antique shop. I commented on how quiet downtown was and we realized it was only 8:00 in the morning.

"I doubt he's open," I was truly disappointed. I wanted to maintain this momentum.

"Well, let's at least go by and see if he has his hours posted," Wally suggested.

"Good idea," I agreed.

We walked two blocks north, turned down a side street, barely more than an alley, and came out on the other side of a back street. There was a short row of specialty shops and a sign that said Dempsy's Antiques and Collectibles with an arrow pointing to the back.

"Are you sure you 'just happened by' this place?" I asked suspiciously.

"Yeah, kind of. Didn't seem this far off the beaten path yesterday," he said totally lacking conviction. Perhaps all this mumbo-jumbo had him doubting himself too.

We finally made it to Dempsy's Antiques and Collectibles and we both stopped short with our mouths hanging open. I put a hand on Wally's arm and started to back away.

The front of the store had broken glass all over the sidewalk. The front window was shattered. The door had been kicked in and hung drunkenly, splintered and battered.

Chapter Twenty-Two

"**W**hat in the hell?" Wally stared at the storefront trying to comprehend the scene.

"Someone wanted in really bad," I said shaking my head. "Let's get out of here!"

"I need to check on the old man," Wally said shaking my hand off his arm.

"Wally, let's call the cops and let them do the investigating. We don't want our fingerprints all over the place," I said being the voice of reason.

"See? That's why you need to go back to the old Red. The old Red would have run into that store," Wally said disapprovingly.

Was he right? Had I become cautious?

"Okay, but don't *touch* anything!" I admonished.

The inside of the store was very dim with darkened corners and deep shadows. The further back we went, the darker it got. Our eyes eventually adjusted and what we saw was heartbreaking. Smashed display cases, collectibles shattered on the floor, and papers strewn as though a tornado had passed through the inside. My heart was pounding in my chest.

Wally found a door in the back of the store. He looked at me with questions in his eyes.

"Leave it," I said, "and let's get out of here. We definitely need to call the police."

"Wait," he said trying the doorknob. Okay, first of all, Wally's prints were going to be on the doorknob, secondly, what if the criminals were behind that door?

Wally gently turned the doorknob and the door swung open. It was an apartment of sorts. Apparently, Mr. Dempsy lived at his store. Wally took a step in with me breathing down his neck.

"Mr. Dempsy?" he called. "Mr. Dempsy, it's Wally. From yesterday?"

Silence. I heard flies buzzing.

"I don't like this," I stage whispered.

"You're making my neck sweat," he retorted. "Back up a little."

I hung back a half pace, but I wasn't about to get too far from him.

"You check that side and I'll check this side," Wally said in his normal voice.

"Wh-what?" I croaked. "By myself?"

Wally looked annoyed.

"Okay, but if some ax murderer jumps out and kills and rapes me, my blood is on your hands!" I grumbled.

I crept quietly into the postage-stamp-sized galley kitchen. I could hear a clock ticking and looked up to see an old black cat clock with his tail ticking off the seconds, eyes darting from one side to the other. Well, that's not creepy. I left the kitchen and saw a door standing open. I peered into the darkness and could just barely make out stairs leading down into a basement. Why was the door open? I felt for a wall switch and locating it, turned on the light. It wasn't a lot of help; the bulb was dull and cast a weak yellow glow. At least, it illuminated the stairs. I quietly made my way down each step, wincing with each squeak of old wood.

I stopped on the bottom step and tried to look into the gloom. Antique dolls lined a narrow shelf. Their blank eyes staring right at me. I took a deep breath and stepped onto the basement floor. Marionettes hung from the ceiling, old dusty books stacked half hazardly, antique farming tools, a mishmash of yesteryear. I couldn't help but wonder what stories this curiosity shop held…I tripped and fell flat on my face, on a body, a cold body. I did what any self-respecting sleuth would do, I screamed like a little girl.

I heard Wally running down the stairs taking two at a time. He stopped at the bottom.

"Red? You okay? Where are you?" he shouted.

I couldn't speak, only some garbled grunting noises as I stood pointing at what I assumed was, poor old Mr. Dempsy.

Wally finally located me and skidded to a stop as he took in the scene.

"Oh, no," he breathed.

"Mr. Dempsy?" I asked totally annoyed that my voice was shaking.

Wally nodded. He put his arms around me and pulled me back. "We need to call the police," he said unnecessarily.

"Duh? Ya think, Sherlock?" I felt like my legs were going to give out. I wanted to sit and catch my breath, but those damned dolls were staring at me like I was next.

"You see that knife sticking out of his chest?" Wally asked as he staggered with me leaning on him.

"What knife?" I asked as the skin on my scalp prickled.

"You didn't see that knife? It was old, really old. I wonder if it was in his stuff. I can't see a killer using an antique

160

knife to kill someone and then leaving it behind," he mused as though he hadn't even heard me.

"Here. You sit here. I want to go take a closer look," he said depositing me on a step so the watchful evil dolls could keep an eye on me.

"No!" I said grabbing his arm. "Let's just go, Wally, I just want to get out of here. Let's go call the police. Let them deal with it."

Wally hesitated, chewing on his lower lip. Eventually, he nodded and helped me up.

We called from Mr. Dempsy's landline because I didn't have a cell phone on me, well, I didn't have…I really needed to get one. Why was I so resistant? Putting it off was no longer an option. One of these days I was going to find myself in a very bad situation and I would have no way of calling for help.

The police arrived and immediately separated us, asking us probing questions.

What were we doing in the basement of an antique shop at this early hour?

What association did we have with the victim?

Had we touched anything?

Did we see anyone suspicious around the store? In the store?

Of course, we had to stick around and give statements.

The cop asked Wally if he knew if anything was missing. Wally explained that he really didn't know Mr. Dempsy. They had a nice conversation yesterday and he was coming by this morning to ask some questions.

"You were coming to ask him some questions before the store opened? About what?" the cop asked giving Wally a suspicious look.

"Well, no, not exactly," Wally said, his face turning pink.

"Well, what exactly then?"

"We were…see, we went to breakfast and…we were just stopping by to see if he had store hours posted," Wally was starting to panic. I wanted to help him out of the hole he was digging, but I really didn't know what to add. I had my own problems. They were asking me pretty much the same questions and I didn't know how to answer. *Yeah, well, you see, officer. Funny thing. I've been seeing these ghosts, see? We are looking for Chuck Doup and his Cadillac, see?* I sounded nuttier and nuttier as the scenario played out.

"And so, you went into the store to see what hours were posted, and you just happened to trip over a dead body, in the basement. Where exactly did you think most stores post their hours?"

I stepped forward, not sure what I was going to say. I liked to be just as surprised as everyone else with what popped out of my mouth.

"Look, officer, we're investigating a story and this guy might have been helpful. We just wanted to talk to him…at some point, and when we got here, we saw the smashed front window and then we got concerned about him, so we went in to check on him," well, that sounded believable.

"Red? Is that you, Red?" I heard a voice behind me. I turned and saw an officer approaching me.

"Don't you remember me? That whole deal with the wolf?" he said with a bright smile.

"Oh, yeah!" as recognition eluded me, "You wanted to shoot my dog!"

The officer laughed and shook his head. "It wasn't a dog, it was a Grey Wolf, but it all worked out, didn't it? You ever name him?"

"Yeah, his name is Spirit Smoke," I said proudly.

162

"Sounds like something you'd name him. Almost didn't recognize you with the new hairdo," he chatted. "Kinda miss the old, though, gotta be honest."

Still smiling, he turned to the investigating cop and said with humor, "I know this girl. She's a bit strange, okay, a whole lot strange, but harmless."

"But..." the cop started.

"I'll vouch for them," the friendly cop said. What was his name? Did I even know his name? I swear I didn't truly recognize him, but I knew Arron and there were two cops there the night they were going to take Spirit away from me, so deductive reasoning said this must have been cop number two. Right?

"Thank you," Wally and I said in unison.

He pointed at me, "You? I know." He pointed at Wally, "You? I have no idea who you are, but if you're with Red, you gotta be okay."

Wally kind of deflated but kept his mouth shut.

"Okay, I think I have enough information. I'll contact you if I have more questions. Don't plan on leaving town any time soon," the cop said snapping his notebook shut. It was pretty obvious he had been embarrassed.

"Hey, Red, how is the wolf doing?" the good cop asked.

"He's doing great!" I said. In my mind I was saying, and guess what? *He's a translator for the dead! Imagine that! Not only can he talk for the dead, but I have a talking wolf!* I decided not to push my luck.

"Thanks so much for asking," I said pleasantly, "Can we go now?"

"Yeah, sure," he said waving us off. "I'll let you know what we find out and if we'll need to talk to you anymore."

"Cool," I said, and we turned to leave, trying not to seem too eager to get the hell out of there.

To say we were quiet on the way back to the car would have been the understatement of the year.

"Good thing that cop knew you," Wally commented. "I sensed things were going south fast."

"I swear, I don't have any idea who that was," I confessed.

"He seemed to know you," he pointed out.

"I know. Kind of made my skin crawl," I mumbled.

When we arrived at my house, I saw a little red scooter drunkenly leaning against the fence. Now what?

I opened the door to Aunt Jo carrying a cup of coffee into the living room. Her eyes glanced over the rim of her cup.

"Either a very late night or a very early morning. Where you two been and why are you up at butt-crack dawn o'clock?"

I stomped into the kitchen to get my own coffee. Breakfast seemed decades ago. I snagged some oatmeal cookies and plopped down at the table.

Wally and I began our tale of the morning.

"Nasty business is all I can say," my Aunt Jo said clucking her tongue. "What *have* you gotten yourself into?"

"Hey, Aunt Jo. I'm really not in the mood right now," I dismissed her.

"Listen to me, you're in way over your head," she warned. "There are things you do not understand and if you keep this up, you're liable to be next."

"How'd...did you have anything to do with this?" I asked as an idea began to take hold. After all, she did say she was my Protector...would she? More importantly, did I have to tell Nice Cop if she did? If he thought I was weird, he definitely was not prepared for my Aunt Jo.

164

"That's not important right now. What's important is giving you a crash course in all things supernatural. And who the hell are YOU?" she whirled on Wally.

Poor Wally faltered a couple of steps back in panic under my Aunt Jo's death ray glare.

"Relax, this is Wally. You might say my partner in crime," I explained while I fumbled getting more cookies out of the box. Not even noon yet and already I was so tired I could barely put one foot in front of the other.

They eyeballed each other like two alley cats squaring off.

"Look, both of you calm down. I'm too tired to referee so you'd just have to kill each other," I sat sulking. Wally plopped down in the dining room chair, still watching my Aunt Jo, just to make sure she wasn't going to attack him while his back was turned. Just to be on the safe side, he took the chair closest to the wall.

Aunt Jo put her cup on the counter. "Well, I'm outta here. Sounds like things might be about ready to heat up."

She adjusted the flaps on her hat, pulled the eye goggles down and breezed out the door. I could hear the putt-putt of the red scooter and last I saw her, she was wobbling and weaving down the road.

"Wow! Who was that? A relative of yours?" he gasped. "I gotta tell ya, that is one scary broad!"

"She's not scary, she's crazy. There's a difference," I snapped.

Yeah, yeah, yeah, first meetings don't always leave the best impressions. I wanted to crawl back into my warm, inviting bed and just forget about seeing my first dead body...not really seeing it but landing on top of it! Sleep, I really, really needed sleep.

Instead, Wally plopped my toboggan on my head and propelled me back out to the car. Crap! Would this morning never end? I looked up dazed and confused. Wally turned into the parking lot of a cell phone store. Now? Really? Seriously, dude!

"The excuses stop now, Red. We're going in to get you a cell phone," he said through a clenched jaw.

Uh-oh, the adrenaline was ebbing, and the anger was setting in. I'd never seen him look so angry.

Like a petulant child, I dutifully followed him into the store.

Chapter Twenty-Three

I decided I must have lived an extremely sheltered life. I'd never seen so many phones of every size and price range in my life! It just boggled my mind. A thousand dollars for this tiny little thing? What call was worth answering on a phone that was no bigger than a pocket notebook?

A very nice, very young clerk approached us with a much too white toothy smile and acne across his cheeks. "What can I help you folks with today?"

Folks? Really, dude?

"We're in the market for a cell phone," Wally stated the obvious. What did he think we were doing here, picking out a sofa? I caught the wink Wally gave the kid as he said, "First time user."

"Ahhhh," the young man nodded. "Been hiding under a rock, have we?"

I gave him a withering glare to which he laughed. "Not to worry! We have quite a few good, reliable phones for you to choose from that are simple to use. Do you know what features you might be interested in?"

I could feel anger starting to bubble in my stomach. I think Wally could sense the temperature rising. He quickly answered for me.

"I think she'd like keyboard texting," he glanced at me. Too late, I had this little twit in my crosshairs. "And maybe a camera…"

"Ahhhh…" the clerk, whose nametag said Shaun, nodded. He was starting to annoy me as he mimicked a bobblehead doll, a bobblehead doll that kept saying *Ahhhhh*.

"Step right over here, ma'am, I'm pretty sure we can fix you right up," he turned to walk to the back of the store and I don't know what came over me, I truly don't, but I have a feeling that on top of everything else that had happened today, ma'am was the proverbial straw that broke the camel's back. I grabbed him by the arm and shoved him against a counter. Wally jumped in to save this kid and I shrugged him off. I got to within an inch of his face while still holding him in a vise grip. The hellhounds had been unleashed and they were on the run with Red the Terrible riding her black steed holding her latest victim's head by the hair.

"Listen, you perky little idiot. We're closer in age than you think so I'm not 'ma'am', do you understand me? I also don't appreciate your smug arrogance just because I've never fed your overblown industry by buying the newest and best cell phone. You know, those little boxes that keep the world connected whether we want to or not? The one that causes people to stop talking to each other? I don't give a rat's ass if it takes pictures, sings the Star-Spangled Banner, or serves me coffee…."

"Actually, Red, you do need a camera," Wally calmly interjected.

I blinked at him, "I do?"

"Yeah, for, you know…things," he said cryptically.

"Ohhh…yeah, I guess you're right," as it dawned on me what 'things' Wally might be referring.

Shaun had the look of a deer in headlights.

"Okay, I want a friggin' device that will make a call as well as receive a call and I guess a camera but none of that other crap. Comprende? That, as you say, rock I've been hiding under? Well, sweetheart, while hiding under that rock, I've seen things that would give you nightmares, and your children nightmares, should there just happen to be a Mrs. Idiot lurking around out there, and their children. Do NOT f..."

"Red!" Wally yelled, breaking the spell.

I stared a second or two longer into the terrified clerk's eyes for dramatic effect before releasing him.

"Have I made myself clear," I made a show of noticing his name tag, "Shaun?"

Shaun was nodding furiously, "Yes, ma'am, I mean, Miss, I mean..."

I patted him on the arm and straightened his shirtfront. "Fine. Now about those phones."

A few minutes later we walked out of the store with me beaming like a moron. I finally owned a cell phone. Had no freaking idea how to use one, but by golly, I had one!

"Geez, Red, you kinda went left in there! You just itchin' to get us arrested today?" Wally fidgeted behind the steering wheel.

"Oh, come on, he had it coming. He called me ma'am! You heard that, right?" I defended myself.

We finally made it home and it never felt so good. I couldn't wait to get inside, close all the curtains and just forget life as I knew it existed. The moment I opened the door, I felt that little bubble pop. I smelled coffee. Wally looked at me with unspoken questions. Too tired to care, I stomped through the doorway and straight into the kitchen.

Yep. There sat Aunt Jo again, who apparently had raided my cabinets and found cookies and dog treats. Spirit was sitting at attention, patiently waiting on his cut of the haul.

"Bout time you got home," she quipped. "Anyone ever tell you; you are way too busy early mornings?"

"Aunt Jo, why are you here again? Twice in one morning? I'm really tired. Can this wait?" I greeted her as I snagged a cookie.

She looked past me and snarled, "Oh. *He's* here?"

"Be nice, Aunt Jo. He's a friend of mine and yes, he's here," I said stonily.

She sniffed and bit into a cookie and tossed Spirit a treat.

"How many of those has he had?" I asked seeing Spirit impatiently waiting for another treat.

"Let's talk about this morning," Aunt Jo said clapping the crumbs from her fingers.

"Let's not and say we did," I refused to give up on my dream of going back to bed and pulling the covers over my head.

"I want to talk about this morning," Wally chimed in.

I gave him 'the look', "Don't you have to go home or something?"

In answer, he pulled up a chair and grabbed the cookie tin. There was nothing but crumbs.

"Nope! Red, we can pretend it didn't happen, we cannot talk about it, but I have questions. Geez, Red, I just talked to that guy yesterday afternoon! Then this morning he's lying in a pool of blood with a dagger through his heart? Hell, yeah, I want to talk about it!"

"Fine," I huffed.

Aunt Jo was looking smug.

"What?" I barked at her. "It was a robbery gone horribly wrong as they sometimes do. No big mystery there. I absolutely refuse to see spooks and goblins around every corner!"

Aunt Jo was zeroed in on Wally, "Dagger?"

Wally nodded, "Yeah. It was black with gold swirly things on it. I couldn't see it real good, but good enough to know it wasn't an everyday kitchen knife. Besides, I never noticed him having any knives at all in his shop. Mostly artifacts from families of yesteryear and old tools."

Aunt Jo studied her folded hands, "Guys, this is getting serious. You are in great danger."

I smiled inwardly at the drama of such a statement, but I knew better than to let it slip to the outside of my face.

All at once, my aunt shot out of her chair and grabbing me by the arm, slapped me across my face. Stunned I fell back a couple of steps and put a hand over my cheek. Before I could react, she grabbed my other arm and brought me close to her face. Her eyes were flashing, her skin flushed, I have to admit, I was scared.

"Probably Magic Sarangoski. It's time you realized this is not a parlor game. This is not an illusion of insanity. This is real, with real dangers, and real death. Your stupidity is going to get you killed and, most certainly, your good friend killed as well. It's time you got down off your high horse and looked around you with some reality. They will never find who broke into that old man's store, they will never possess that knife, it's gone. There is no killer to be brought to justice. Think about that and let that sink in," she paused. "There are forces at work, dark forces, light forces, demons, and angels. They are here among us; everyone is vulnerable to them. However, there are a select few, who are chosen to try to maintain some

172

semblance of order between those two forces. I'm real, and sorry, princess, but you're one of them. We don't ask to be chosen, we have no control over it, but you answer your calling, or you join the dark force.

"Now, think! What could Rocco have been looking for?"

Silence settled over the small kitchen as Aunt Jo bore her gaze right to the very center of my soul.

Wally cleared his throat discreetly. We both looked at him. He raised his hand tentatively.

"What?" we said in unison.

"I think I may have an idea," he croaked.

Neither of us invited him to continue, so he kind of waited a moment and then said meekly, "If you're sure it was Rocco, well, I was in that store yesterday talking to the old man about Chuck Doup and that night he and his friends disappeared. He showed me the newspaper clipping and said that wasn't the whole story."

He looked to me for help, but I didn't offer.

"I came over this morning to tell Red about it," he said nodding toward me seeking validation.

"And?" Aunt Jo said.

At least he was taking the focus off me. I felt my world crashing down on me, the full weight of it making my knees weak. I sank down into the nearest chair.

Poor Wally was trapped now. His eyes followed me as I sat, trying to catch my breath.

"You okay, Red?"

Aunt Jo cast a quick glance at me, "She's fine. Explain yourself."

"Well, I was telling Red, I was just wandering around downtown and happened on this antique store. Dempsy's

Antiques and Collectibles. I was looking in the window when I saw a really old pair of eyeglasses. I stepped inside, and I really don't know why except it just seemed like the thing to do. I asked about them and we got to talking. I noticed a framed newspaper clipping hanging up behind the counter. It was about the night Chuck disappeared. Mr. Dempsy said he went to school with Chuck and that people didn't know the whole story behind that night. I asked him what the whole story was. To make a long story short, apparently, Chuck and his friends found a chest full of money. We think it may be Peter Euclid's treasure. In it was a note that was kind of cryptic."

"What did it say?" Aunt Jo demanded, clearly impatient with how long the story was taking.

Wally didn't have a chance to answer. Suddenly all the lights went out. The temperature dropped, leaving a chill in the air. It became dark in the little cottage.

Aunt Jo put a finger to her lips. "He's here," she whispered.

Chapter Twenty-Four

We sat in total silence. I'm not sure I could testify in a court of law that I was breathing. I have never felt such fear in my life. In my peripheral vision, I watched a shadow slide across the walls. A lamp flickered a couple of times. I heard books falling from the bookcase, I heard an outlet short out, with the briefest of sparks. Cushions on the sofa flipped off, papers fluttered angrily. The shadow came to the kitchen door and stood facing us. Now, I could testify in a court of law that I was not breathing.

The shadow stood there for a moment. Watching? Listening?

All at once, a huge shape launched at the specter. The shadow tried to flee back into the living room. I heard unholy, guttural growls, whimpers, and attacking teeth snapping. Spirit was fighting the shadow, protecting us. Aunt Jo used the distraction to stand and outstretch her arms, her head thrown back, eyes closed. Slowly she raised her arms above her head until the palms met. A smoky blue aura emanated from her and gently surrounded the table. She turned and pointed to the living room. A blue glow exposed the shadow and like the black smoke from burning oil, the shadow vanished.

The lights came back on. Wally and I sat in stunned incredulity. Aunt Jo's shoulders slumped, and she dropped her head.

I felt paralyzed. I felt violated, all my senses assaulted, leaving me weak and disoriented.

"HOLY CRAP ON A CRACKER!" Wally screeched three octaves higher than his normal voice. I looked at him dazed and confused. "What the…how…holy crap on a cracker!"

"You saw that?" I asked once I could find my voice.

"Frickin' yeah!" he said taking a shaky deep breath.

Aunt Jo finally regained her composure and sat at the table with us. She looked pale and drained. "That wasn't Rocco," she said as worry etched her face.

We all jumped when there was frantic pounding on the door.

"Now what?" I grumbled.

I opened the door to a wild-eyed Miss Vera.

"Are you guys okay?" she asked rushing through the doorway.

"Come in and join the pow-wow," I said leading the way to the kitchen.

Wally was gushing over Aunt Jo and her power. She didn't appear to hear him. No doubt the concerns in her head drowning out a human voice.

Miss Vera sat in my chair, so I took the seat next to Wally.

"What happened to your hair, Red?" he asked.

Everyone turned their eyes to me.

"What?" putting my hand self-consciously to my hair.

"You have a white streak in it," Wally said pointing to my forehead.

Spirit limped into the kitchen holding a front paw up. I rushed to him. He looked at me with pleading eyes.

"Spirit's hurt!"

Miss Vera came to him and spoke softly. He allowed her to hold him and examine his leg.

"Nothing seems to be broken," she said with relief. "Please tell me what happened."

Aunt Jo sighed and shook her head. "We had a visitor."

Miss Vera barely breathed, "Who?"

"Brendore," she answered simply.

"Who's Brendore?" I asked. The cast of characters in this story just kept getting bigger and bigger. I felt myself being sucked into the vortex of a world I didn't understand and didn't want.

The two women ignored me. "I'm sure he's responsible for the death of the old man this morning," Aunt Jo reasoned.

"Oh, my, that's not good. Not good at all," Miss Vera was shaking her head.

"Who's Brendore and why is he threatening us?" I asked with more urgency. I could tell by the way Vera and Jo were acting, this was some serious business.

"Brendore is a dark forces overlord," Aunt Jo explained. "He's kind of, what you would say, Rocco's boss. He's after something, something he thinks is very important. Probably, think child. What has happened that would call the dark forces?"

I chewed on my lip in concentration. "I have no idea, Aunt Jo. I haven't been able to make sense out of any of this. We thought it might be Peter's treasure, but what in heaven's name would ghosts want with money?"

Wally had been sitting silent all this time. Definitely out of his league, I wouldn't blame him one bit if he left and never came back.

"What if it isn't the money per se? What if the money was a means to an end?" he asked looking at each of us, as the wheels in his head whirred and clanked, trying to find the common groove. "Do you have paper and pencil, Red?"

I had no idea.

"Look in the drawer beneath the bookshelf," Miss Vera suggested.

Wally looked as though going into that living room was the last thing he wanted to do. Can't say that I blamed him. Spirit understood and rose to escort him. We heard him rummaging around and then he was back with the supplies.

"Okay, Red, remember in class they were talking about every action having a reaction? You know, marketing one way has a reaction and marketing a different way having a total lack of reaction? It's where the statistical data comes in handy. You're better able to tell what marketing strategy has the best chance of garnering the most revenue." He was on a roll as the cogs came closer and closer to the common groove.

When no response came, he pushed on, "Okay. This all started when Peter gave you the letter."

"Yeah, I'm supposed to give it to a woman whose been dead for over two hundred years," I said sarcastically.

"Maybe not," he said thoughtfully. "What if it's something to do *with* the letter and not the letter itself?"

"What do you mean?" Miss Vera was definitely interested now.

"Maybe we've been going at this all wrong," he replied. "I saw a documentary one time where they talked about spies back in the Civil War used something like invisible ink to smuggle messages out. What if there is a message in the letter that we can't see?"

"Like what?" I asked.

"I don't know. See, we've been looking for Chuck and the Cadillac and the money. You pointed out that it would go to Rosa's family anyway so why all the hoopla in the spirit world?" he pondered. "It must have something to do with the family itself. Do you have the letter, Red?"

I stood to retrieve the letter, "I don't want to damage it in any way. Lydia Jackson will be here in a couple of weeks..."

I didn't have a chance to finish my sentence. Aunt Jo's head jerked up. "Who?"

"Lydia Jackson. She's a relative of Rosa's. A great-great-great aunt or something like that."

"Lydia Jackson died a few years back," she said flatly.

I stood dumbfounded. "But I talked to her! She's coming out here to retrieve the letter!"

Aunt Jo shook her head. "Impossible. I remember Lydia Jackson. She was plastered all over the newspapers. She was desperate to find the money Peter supposedly left behind. As a matter of fact, there were rumors that Lydia got pregnant as a teenager and disappeared for a while. When she got back, there was no baby and no one ever spoke of it. She became obsessed with finding that money. I don't know who is coming to get the letter, but it is not Lydia Jackson."

"But Chuck and his friends found it!" I said really not following the thread Aunt Jo used to weave the theory.

"Okay. So, there is something that connects that letter to Peter's treasure," she surmised.

We sat lost in our own thoughts.

"Is that...thing...coming back?" I asked dreading the answer.

"Yes," Aunt Jo answered bluntly. "And we need to find Brendore's connection in all of this. He's a very powerful overlord. He represents greed and selfishness. Very powerful, indeed. I tend to think that Rocco may have enlisted Brendore's help, or Brendore saw an opportunity for himself."

"Again, I ask, having yet to get a straight answer, WHY are all these spirits wanting this money so bad?"

"I think someone invited them into their life. Trust me, humans by their very nature are greedy and selfish. If I had to guess, I'd say that whoever is posing as Lydia Jackson, has something to gain from finding that money. Family love has nothing to do with it," Aunt Jo finished with a disgusted look on her face.

I realized I hadn't eaten since breakfast early this morning. Here it was, fully dark and along with being famished to the point of starvation, I was physically and mentally drained. Not one extra ounce of energy left. It had been a very, very long day.

"I don't mean to be rude, but I'm hungry and tired," I said putting my hands on my hips. "Does anyone else want something to eat? And then I'm going to bed."

They blinked at me in surprise.

"I'll help you throw something together," Wally offered.

"I have a roast that's been simmering all afternoon," Miss Vera volunteered.

"Awesome. Wally and I will put together a salad and some garlic bread," I said finally taking charge just as the old me would do.

Miss Vera went to get her roast beef while Wally and I chopped and diced. I fed Spirit, who was all too ready to eat, but still a little disappointed there weren't more treats coming his way. He had been laying in his bed listening to us talk. I saw his eyes flutter a couple of times. Poor baby was also exhausted and sore and hungry. My heart nearly broke with the love I had for him. I knelt down to him and put my arms around him.

"Thank you for protecting us," I whispered. He laid his big head against my shoulder and sighed.

We ate, I would like to say in silence because my head was feeling like an overblown balloon as I struggled to sort out and understand what had happened in the course of one day, but no, there was conversation, lots of it. I tuned it out. I just could not physically take any more in. I just wanted to eat and then crawl between the sheets hugging my wolf and drift off to sleep.

Aunt Jo helped me clear the table. Wally and Miss Vera did the dishes. When the kitchen was cleaned up, I announced, "If anyone needs a place to stay the night, feel free to use whatever you can. Linens are in the hall closet; pillows are in the storage room. Goodnight."

What on earth was I thinking? Sleep was not on the agenda, at least, not right away. I was ashamed that I was actually afraid to go to sleep. I didn't want the boogeyman to catch me at my most vulnerable.

Chapter Twenty-Five

The sun pried my reluctant eyes open. I hoped it was all a dream. As I shuffled into the kitchen to put the coffee on, I realized it was very quiet. Maybe it was a dream, after all! The coffee aroma was intoxicating and breathing the caffeine aroma I felt all was right with the world. A tousled Wally appeared in the kitchen doorway.

"Ah, just what I need," he said, his voice still sleepy.

"You stayed here last night?" I stated the obvious.

"Yeah, listen Red, I need to talk to you about something, but coffee first," he nodded.

My hope of waking from a dream quickly evaporated.

Lacking energy for anything more ambitious, I set out a couple of cereal boxes and bowls.

He took a bowl and shook cereal in it. He went to the fridge and got the milk as though he did this, in my house, as a matter of routine. I had a sinking feeling in the pit of my stomach.

"It really did happen, didn't it?" I asked hoping against hope.

With a mouthful of Cap'n Crunch and milk dribbling down his chin, he nodded.

"It was wild!"

"Wally? I'm not sure I'm up for this. What if I'm not strong enough? What if I just screw things up even more?"

Wally rested his arm on the table, "Red, you are the strongest woman I know. You're smart, tough, and not afraid to kick butt. You are strong enough and just remember, even the strongest knot can be untangled. You can do this. I'll be your sidekick! Batman had Robin, Indiana Jones had Short Round, The Little Mermaid had Sebastian and Red has Wally."

I couldn't help it, I giggled at the thought of having a sidekick. "And Sherlock Holmes had Dr. Watson."

He laughed too and turned serious. "Your Aunt Jo may be crazy, but she's one tough cookie. I couldn't believe what I was seeing last night. She's also right. We are slowly wading out into dangerous waters. We've got to get this figured out before someone else gets hurt or killed."

He was right, of course. Maybe Wally wasn't so much my sidekick, as the one who kept me grounded. He kept me focused. He believed in me more than I believed in myself. He treated Mr. Dempsy's death as a tragedy of this mission, I treated it like an inconvenience. It was time to grow up, I told myself.

I sat at the table with him, hugging my coffee cup. I watched him eat for a minute while lost in my own thoughts.

"So, where do we go from here? I have a feeling we haven't seen the last of that demon, what was his name?" I asked through the fog of last night.

"Brendore," he answered. "Nasty fella."

"That's true. I don't even want to think what would have happened without Spirit and Aunt Jo. He was looking for something though. What was he looking for? I find it hard to believe a demon would exit the depths of hell, commit murder, and aggressively pursue, all for a love letter," I wondered out loud.

"Well, the way I see it, we're missing some critical link. It goes back to making sure Rosa gets the letter. I'm beginning to think this Lydia Jackson is part of the puzzle, and not a good part," he said as he stood to rinse his bowl and pour a cup of coffee. "At least we know it's not really Lydia Jackson, but someone or some*thing* posing as her, to get whatever it is they're after."

"Aunt Jo and Miss Vera both said she was adamant about finding the money. What if she's the reason that Brendore demon showed up?" I asked.

"Didn't you say you researched the family tree?" he returned to his seat and yawned.

"Yeah, I did, but I have to admit that as soon as I found a living relative, I quit and contacted Lydia right away. Maybe there's more to the story than that," I guessed.

"Okay, so I say we go a little further and deeper on that. You said Lydia was due to be here in a couple of weeks?"

"Yeah," I exclaimed as I realized an entire day had melted away. Holy crap!

"Okay, so we've got less than two weeks to look for the missing piece," he said.

"Don't forget, we still don't know where the money is, either," I reminded him.

"Don't say anything to Lydia about the money and whatever you do, don't give her that letter. It needs to be put in a safe place until we can get all this sorted out," he advised me. He was right again.

"You said you wanted to talk to me about something?" I remembered him saying.

"Yeah, I'm moving in with you," he stood and scratched his belly. "Well, I'm in the shower."

I sat there with my mouth hanging open. "Wait! What?" I cried leaping from my chair.

I heard the water in the shower. Move in with me? How did…when…oh, hell no! I work alone! Whatever that meant. I marched into the bathroom and perched on the bathroom counter. The water turned off and a hand reached around the shower curtain for a towel. I handed it to him. He was a bit surprised to see me sitting there. As he began to step out, I stretched a leg out, blocking him.

"Uh-uh. You don't say something like that and walk away!" I admonished him. "I don't recall us ever having that particular discussion and who says I *want* you to move in with me?"

He looked at my foot braced against the wall. He gently put his hand out and removed it. I about fell off my perch. He smiled.

"That was before last night. Red, I saw everything! I SAW it! Haven't you stopped to wonder why? I didn't see the guy at the fountain, I haven't seen this Peter dude, but I saw everything last night. The shadow, the papers flying around, the blue aura, Spirit suddenly turning into a rabid wolf to protect us. I sat during the conversation with your Aunt Jo and Vera. Why?" I didn't have an answer. Now, thinking about it, *why was he able to see everything?*

"I am not going to sit around and worry about you. I don't want to come to see you and find you in a pool of blood with an antique knife in your chest. If one is strong, two will be stronger," he finished.

He had me there. I didn't have any arguments, at least not yet. He removed his towel, put it back on the towel rack and walked buck naked out of the bathroom. Didn't even occur to me to look. I'm really not a girly-girl.

I remained sitting on the bathroom counter for a minute or two, just thinking about what just happened. He made valid points. I wondered if he would see Peter the next time he appeared. Spirit wandered in. He wasn't limping this morning, that was a good sign. I ruffled his neck fur and looked into his eyes. "What do you think?" I asked him. I swear I saw him smile. A whole new level of a wolfish grin.

I went into the living room where Wally sat looking through my genealogy file.

"Okay, ground rules," I said without preamble. "First, you sleep on the couch."

"Fine," he mumbled.

"Secondly, stay out of my personal space," I wasn't sure what that meant exactly, but it seemed pretty lame to have just one ground rule.

"Oh, and you have to share in household chores. Taking out the trash, walking Spirit, doing the dishes, you know, stuff like that."

"Fine. Any more rules?"

"Not at this time, but I'll think of more," I said weakly. I think I won this particular battle, but I wasn't sure. I didn't have the winners rush.

Wally tapped the paper in front of him, "I'm seeing a bit of a gap here."

"What do you mean?" I asked as I went to look over his shoulder.

"Well, according to the family tree. Rosa was born in 1846. She was the sixth child out of twelve. There was a sister who was older than her, born in 1820. Marjorie."

"Yeah, so? I followed that up but it dead-ended," I informed him.

"Red, people don't just disappear. Mind if I take this?" holding up the paper.

"Take it where?" I asked.

"I have a friend I want to take a look at this. He's a genius on this stuff. He can find out history like no one else I know. I'll make sure we get it back. I don't know why, but it bugs me. There's no marriages for either Rosa or Marjorie, no date of death, no children, nothing. There has to be a reason."

I felt a strange prickle on the back of my neck. One of the missing pieces?

"Okay. Sure," I agreed.

He gathered up all the papers and replaced them in the file. On impulse, he stood and gave me a peck on the cheek. "See ya later. Spirit, you take care of our girl, okay?"

I was surprised at how empty the house felt once he left. I decided to take a quick shower. Macho Man may feel perfectly free to parade around in the suit God gave him, but I certainly wasn't. Oh, there's another rule. Wear pants...at all times.

The shower was heavenly and anything but quick. I allowed the water to rinse away all the uncertainty of the past few days. I allowed it to soak my hair, run over my breasts, and take all that grime and guilt and disappear into the drain. I reached for the shampoo that made my hair silky and shiny and then stopped. Instead, I used my old brand. I scrubbed from head to toe until my skin was pink. As I stepped out, I took a rare moment and looked in the fogged-up mirror. Did I really want to see what I would see?

I grabbed a fresh towel and wiped the glass clean. My hair hung wet and heavy in spiral curls. It came to just below my shoulders. There was the white streak. It didn't look too imposing. My face looked different. Maybe more mature, or more like someone who had seen things that most didn't see. My green eyes were bright and the same grass green, but now I noticed gold flecks in them. Had they always been there? A thought skipped through my mind like a rock skipping across a lake only to disappear as quickly as it had sailed. How much had last night changed me?

I had just pulled a t-shirt over my head when I heard a knock on the door. The peace I felt in the shower went down the drain of despair as I dreaded who may be on the other side of the door. Spirit was close on my heels as I padded to the door.

An older lady stood on my step. She was birdlike with beady eyes and a mouth in a permanent frown. I could tell it was permanent by the deep wrinkles along her upper lip and at the corners of her mouth.

"You Probably Sarangoski?" she asked.

"Yeah," I said dumbly.

"I'm Lydia Jackson," she said. "You have something that belongs to me?"

Chapter Twenty-Six

"**Y**ou weren't supposed to be here for another couple of weeks!" Spirit had followed me to the door and was pressed against my side.

"Well, I'm here today," she huffed. "I'll be taking that letter now and be on my way."

I looked at her and decided right away I didn't like her. Her eyes were like flint and darted first one way and the other. She kept licking her lips and she clasped her pocketbook in front of her in a death grip. Spirit seemed to not like her either.

"Please, come in. I wasn't expecting you so soon, so I didn't have it readily accessible," I told her, wondering how I could stall or get rid of her.

"Can I get you a cup of tea?" I asked pleasantly enough.

"No. Just the letter and I'll be gone," she said in a tone that might have been threatening.

"Yes, well, I was hoping to maybe learn more about Peter and Rosa. Theirs is quite the love story," I tried to coax her.

"Not my circus, not my monkeys. The letter, please," she said impatiently.

"I'm sorry, of course," I turned to go to the bookcase and got down Tinsdales Guide to Telemarketing. "I kept it in the most boring book I own. I mean, really, a book on telemarketing? How to be obnoxious in five easy steps?" I gave a little laugh, but Ol' Lydia just fidgeted like she had eaten rocket fuel for breakfast.

"Yeah, well, ahem," I thumbed through the pages until I got to page 126. No letter. I was sure I put it in there! Maybe it was page 216. I fanned the pages. No letter. Baffled, I looked at Lydia who was pursing her lips even more.

"I'm so sorry! I could have sworn I put that letter in here...on page 126!" I apologized.

"Listen, young lady, you do not want to mess with me," that was an out and out threat. Instead of being scared of her, I immediately felt anger start a slow burn.

"You know? I don't think I can help you after all," I said and replaced the book on the shelf.

She rushed me, pushing me out of the way, and began taking books off the shelf, fanning the pages and tossing them to the floor. Come to think of it, Brendore did the same thing last night and he didn't find it either. Sure, I was worried about it not being in my 'safe place', but at the same time, I suspected someone was watching out for me. Spirit's muscles were tensed and ready to spring into action. I saw what he did with that shadow thing, I really didn't want to see what he could do with an 'actual' person.

Hair disheveled, panting, and eyes looking like storm clouds, she turned to me. Her voice was low and hard as granite. "That is my property. The fact that you have it and won't return it to me, means you're stealing from me. I will call the authorities, believe me."

I hoped I looked casual and unconcerned as I sat in an armchair. I smiled at her, "Oh come on, Ms. Jackson. We both know it's not the letter you're after. I know all about your obsessive search for Peter's hidden money. I also know about

Marjorie. Why did she disappear all these years ago? What is your family secret?"

Lydia's face went from pale to white. Her lips twitched; her face carved from stone. "You're in way over your head, young lady. You're dealing with things you are not equipped to deal with. Be a shame if something tragic happened."

"Seriously? You're threatening me?" I chided.

In answer, she stormed out of the house. When she reached the end of the walkway, she turned, "This isn't over!"

I waved at her and shut the door. Holy Crapola on a cracker! On shaking legs that threatened to buckle under me, I held on to furniture and walls to get to a chair. My breath was coming in pants and my vision blurred. That woman was crazy scary! I kind of wished for Brendore. Spirit took up lookout at the window, hackles raised, eyes locked on the woman making her getaway.

I don't know how long I sat there trying to get my bearings. Wally came through the door with a triumphant smile on his face, which disappeared the moment he saw me.

"What happened?" he asked rushing to me.

"Lydia Jackson is here," I replied.

He looked around, "Here?"

"She was here, she left. She threatened me. I think you were right though; I think we need to look closer at Marjorie," I said.

"Are you okay?" he asked, and I could plainly see the concern in his face.

"Yeah, just a little shook up. I'm fine though." Amazingly, I *was* fine. Shook up, yeah, but also feeling like I'd gotten a little closer to finding the complete picture. "What did you find out?"

He hesitated only a heartbeat and sat across me to tell me his news. "Okay, that guy I was telling you about, I don't want to say his name out loud, because we don't know who may be lurking around and the last time, I mentioned a name, it didn't end well. Anyway, I took your notes and gave them to him. He pecked on the keyboard some and then made a couple of calls. He gave me some leads to follow. Here's what he said.

Marjorie was the oldest of twelve children, Rosa was the sixth. Apparently, Marjorie got pregnant out of wedlock and was disowned by the family. She was removed from any future listings. The interesting part is that when Marjorie left, Rosa went with her. Because she was taking care of her sister and not pregnant herself, she was allowed to stay in the family Bible, so to speak."

I felt a light bulb light up over my head. "Unless it wasn't Marjorie who had the baby! What if Rosa had the baby? Since you found out Peter wasn't killed in the Civil War, what if they met in secret?"

Wally looked up at me with the most surprised look, and then I saw the light bulb light up for him. "Geez, Red! What if? It would all tie together then! Go get the letter! Let's see if there's a clue we overlooked."

Oh, oh, oh, how do I tell him I lost the letter? "Didn't you take it?" I asked lamely.

"No, I didn't see any value in it. Does this mean you can't find it?" I could hear the panic in his voice.

"Well, I put it in a book, but it wasn't there," I tried to explain as calmly as I could.

He just sat looking at me. I began to feel pretty uncomfortable.

"Do you think somehow that Jackson woman took it?" he asked.

"I don't think so. I was right there. She or her hands were never out of my sight."

"Then it has to be around here somewhere. I'll help you look for it. We need it now more than ever."

We looked all afternoon. We removed sofa cushions, got down on the floor with flashlights and looked under furniture. We pulled tables and chairs out and looked behind them. We went through every book in the bookshelves, in closets, every kitchen cabinet, and drawer. There very simply was no letter, anywhere. My heart began to sink as I thought of Peter entrusting me with it and me in turn, losing it. I simply did not know where else to look. Wally came in with a frustrated look.

"Well, it isn't in either of our cars," he announced coming into the living room.

"Wally, I have no earthly idea where it is!" I felt like I was going to cry.

He came to me and wrapped me in his arms, "Shhhhh…it will show up. We know one thing for sure, it didn't grow legs and walk out of here."

I pulled back, "Are you sure? I mean, really, I don't know who or what to trust anymore. If ghosts commit murder, ransack houses, and walk among us, why can't letters grow legs and walk out?"

"You're upset," he cooed.

Spirit suddenly stood up with ears cocked. Now what?

He walked to the door and stood at attention.

"Quick! Turn out the lights!" I pushed Wally toward the wall switch. Spirit whined.

"Is it that woman?" Wally whispered.

As my eyes adjusted to the dimness, I saw the faint outline of a military uniform.

"Peter!" I cried.

196

Peter stepped forward and held out his hand. In it, he held the letter.

"Oh, Peter! Thank you! You were the one keeping it safe! If I could, I'd give you a big hug about now," I said feeling the tears closer than ever. "Peter, why can't we talk? I have so many questions!"

Wally stepped forward. I thought he could see Peter's outline. "Did you and Rosa have a child?"

Peter frowned, hung his head and if you weren't watching closely, you would have missed the nod.

I rushed to comfort him, "It's okay, Peter, we aren't judging you. We're trying to make sure the right person gets your letter. Was the money for the child? Was it a daughter or a son?"

Instead, he faded more and more until he vanished.

I sat trying to absorb this new information. So, Peter and Rosa did meet up and felt they had to do it in secret. Why the secrecy? Was Rosa too young in her family's eyes? Did they consider Peter unfit for their daughter? As usual, there were more questions than answers. And, let's say, there was upfront, out in the open, answers, it still didn't make sense trying to get a letter and a treasure chest to a long-dead woman.

"I wonder why they kept things so quiet?" I asked aloud.

"Because Peter was a confederate soldier and Rosa's father was a spy for the Union Army," Spirit said perfectly attuned to the conversation.

Wally fainted and fell off his chair.

It took me a good ten minutes to revive poor Wally. Finally, his eyes fluttered open.

"What...how...did I just...?" he stuttered. Spirit stood over him panting and Wally fainted again.

Poor guy sure has had his world turned upside down since he met me. Which, I think I finally accepted, I'm really not like all the other girls. Now, if we could just get this mystery solved before my best friend has a fatal heart attack, we'd be doing good.

I struggled, yanked, and pulled Wally into the bedroom and managed to get him on the bed. To be kind of smaller than me, the boy packed some serious weight! I was sweating and my back felt like it was breaking, but I did it. I figured I'd just let him sleep it off. Maybe he would think it was all a dream, meanwhile, I had a convoluted mystery to solve.

I went to my desk and pulled out paper and a pencil. I made three columns, no, wait, four columns. Each had a heading that I hoped led us to a conclusion.

1.Characters
2. Relationships
3.Facts (Keep all documentation)
4.Theories

I began to fill in the columns. Eventually, I began to see a pattern emerge. I got more and more excited. I was beginning to see the whole picture. Spirit stood and went to the bedroom door. I turned to see Wally standing in the doorway with his hand on the back of his head.

"I have a headache. Why do I have a headache? More importantly, why do I have a goose egg on the back of my head?" he mumbled.

"I would have thought your first question would be why you woke up in my bed," I smiled.

"Oh, yeah. Why *did* I wake up in your bed?" Poor guy couldn't keep the hope out of his voice or his eyes.

"Don't you remember?" I asked him mischievously. "A night of torrid pleasure and blindingly amazing sex, and you don't remember?"

"Oh my God!" he dropped his hand and his eyes were wide and dilated. "Oh…I am so sorry, Red! I just remember…" he went back into the bedroom and sat on the bed. When I went in, I saw him sitting there shaking his head.

"Oh, relax, nothing happened," I laughed.

His face turned a bright red, what could I do, but hug him?

"You know it happens to guys every once in a while," he said softly.

It was my turn to blink in confusion, then it hit me.

"Oh, no! Not *that*! The whole night never happened. I was just kidding with you. No, you fell off the kitchen chair, that's how you got the bump on your head," I explained hoping we could just leave it at that.

"You mean, I was just sitting there and then all at once, *Whump!* I fell off the chair? Why would I fall off the kitchen chair? Red? What's going on?" he asked pitifully.

"Okay, so we're going to do this right now," I gave a big sigh and sat on the bed with him and recapped the events of the evening.

Chapter Twenty-Seven

He didn't say a word. He just got up from the bed and meandered into the living room and got his blankets for the couch. He brushed his teeth, took some aspirin, and lay on the couch pulling the covers over his head.

"So, I really did hear Spirit talk? It wasn't you messing with me?" I heard the muffled question.

"Yes, Spirit can talk…sometimes. I haven't quite figured out the mechanics yet, but Aunt Jo called him a Translator. No, it wasn't me messing with you," I said, trying to be gentle and understanding.

"So, what we have here, is an Aunt who has superpowers, an old woman who runs a creepy bookstore, a talking wolf, a demon who runs around scaring the shit out of people, and a lunatic dried up old hag willing to kill for money that belongs to a dead woman," he said trying to put the entire incident in some kind of order that would make sense.

I nodded, "That sounds about right."

I felt sorry for him. I didn't have a choice for this kind of life, but he did. He could walk away and go on with his happy, predictable life and forget any of this even happened. Maybe I could get Aunt Jo or somebody to cast some kind of spell to totally erase the memories. That's what they did in the movies.

"Wally, I know all this is beyond comprehension. Heck, I'm still trying to figure it out. I don't have a choice, well, I do, but the options are slim to none. However, you can walk away. Honey, I wouldn't blame you. You did not sign up for this when you said you wanted to be my friend. No hard feelings whatsoever on my part. You wouldn't believe just how understanding I would be if you did," I wanted to lay it all out for him. Give him the chance to exit with dignity.

His head jerked up and he actually looked hurt I would suggest such a thing!

"You want me to leave?"

"No! I like having you around. It's kind of like having two pets instead of one! I'm just saying I would understand if you did."

He rose from the couch and walked toward me with such a look on his face that I took a couple of steps back. He raised a finger and wagged it in front of my face. "First of all, no, I'm not leaving you to deal with this on your own. Second, you need me. After all, who in the world are all these demons going to toss around like rag doll if I'm not around? You? You wouldn't last one round with them! Ha!" he stopped his tirade long enough to put his finger down and added, "I know I've spent a lot of time unconscious lately, but that'll get better, I promise."

"Well. Okay, then," I said for lack of anything else to say.

We stood in awkward silence, inspecting the floor, not quite willing to be the first for eye contact. He took a few steps forward and pulled me into his arms. His hand cupped the back of my head and his other hand rested on the small of my back, pushing me into his kiss.

His kiss. Long, sweet, tender, my first real kiss. I got dizzy, everything melted away except the now. His mouth was soft, warm, and his breath was coming in ragged pants and I trembled. His tongue…his tongue…I pushed him away and glared at his betrayal.

"Geez Louise, Wally! What the hell was that?" I screeched.

He looked a bit confused, "A French Kiss?"

"You stuck your yucky tongue in my mouth!" I protested.

"That's what a French Kiss is, you moron," he snapped.

"Well, no more of that! New ground rule, no kissing with your icky tongue!" I shouted, fighting the urge to run to the bathroom and gargle with antiseptic. I had never felt anything so disgusting in my life!

Well, Wally's feelings were hurt. Wearing only his pajama bottoms, he stormed out of the house. Fine by me!

Wally wasn't the only one confused. Spirit stood looking from one to the other trying to decide if I was in any danger. Wally was his friend too. Would a friend hurt a friend? In the end, he decided to let us fight it out and went to curl up on my bed. I have to say, I thought he'd be a bit more protective.

It was early morning when I heard the front door open. I was still wrestling with guilt. The kiss was so nice. Who am I kidding? It was magical. It made my tummy tickle, an increase in my heart rate, a weakness in my knees. I also felt relief. Relief that he didn't leave me, he came back after he'd cooled off. I turned over to my side and realized I was smiling. Could Probably Magic Sarangoski be falling in love?

When I finally got out of bed, the sun was shining brightly and it was promising to be a cold, crisp day. I made a big breakfast as a peace offering to Wally. It really was a silly spat, that tongue thing just caught me off guard. One could say, I was not well educated in the romance department. To have such hippie-dippie parents, I, myself, had spent my life fighting first one thing and another. Sarcasm, alienation, isolation, those were things I excelled at. Being someone's love interest, not so much. Can you imagine my surprise when I finally realized, I had led an extremely sheltered and protected life?

Wally was led to the kitchen by his nose. I set the platter of bacon on the table and stood back to admire my handiwork. Waffles, fresh strawberries, whipped cream, bacon, apple juice, I gotta say, I impressed myself.

"Good morning!" I chirped.

He gave me an uncertain look, "What's all this?"

"It's I'm-sorry waffles and I-was-an- ass breakfast," I replied as I sat and started spearing waffles.

"No need to apologize," he said, "I don't know what even happened. It wasn't like I planned it or anything. If anyone should apologize, it should be me. I'm sorry, the whole thing was just a mistake."

I felt the air rush out of my happy bubble like a tire that ran over a ten-penny nail.

"A mistake?"

"Yeah. Red, you told me at the very beginning, no hanky-panky. I crossed the line."

I thought about that. He was right, of course. I made sure he understood I fully intended to keep a distance between us, both physical and emotional. I think I was scared of the rejection, but that kiss…I'd never felt so ethereal in all my life. I, in truth, wouldn't mind it happening again. I wondered if he felt the same way.

"So, I have to ask, how was it for you?" I asked.

He shrugged, "It was okay."

"Okay? It was just okay?" I could hear my voice raise a couple of octaves. "My first ever kiss was just okay?"

Wally shrugged again. "Red, all I know is that since I first saw you walk across campus, I've wanted to kiss you. As I've gotten to know you, I've wanted to kiss you, make love to you, keep you safe. Then when it happened, I don't know, things shifted. I don't know how to explain it, but you're right, we need to keep it to ourselves. Again, I'm sorry."

I slammed my fork down and stalked off to my room. My appetite completely gone, my ego completely destroyed, my feelings completely in an uproar. I slammed my bedroom door and sat on my bed fuming. I decided I needed to focus on our mission. The last thing I needed was to complicate things even more by letting my feelings get the better of me. I yanked on my jeans and pulled a t-shirt over my head. I bent to tie my shoe and I began to cry. It was a quiet cry. Not an ugly cry, just a cry full of embarrassment, rejection, and the damned confusion of what I was supposed to do with these strange and misunderstood feelings. When I felt a little more in control, I was ready to face Wally again.

"So, what's on the agenda today?" he asked as I came back into the kitchen. I picked up my water bottle and filled it with cold water.

"I'm going to go look for Chuck's car," I said matter-of-factly.

"Good. Where?"

"I have no idea, but I figure if we retrace the route, maybe something will pop out at us."

"Okay, but you do realize, that route has been retraced a thousand times, right?" he said being perfectly reasonable.

I thought a minute. There was something just on the fringes of my mind. It was like trying to catch a butterfly. I could see it; I just couldn't catch it.

"Yeah, I know. But I'm wondering if everyone keeps retracing the same route. Kind of like watching the same scene in a TV show over and over hoping for a different ending." I leaned against the kitchen counter. "What if Chuckie and his friends didn't end up in the river? What if the car had enough momentum to actually land on the other side?"

"That's an interesting idea," he conceded as he mulled over the possibilities in his mind. "And maybe, where they think the car left the road, wasn't really where it happened," he added.

"Well, I would think if it went into the river, they would have found it sooner or later," I pointed out. "That river rises and then recedes to nothing. It would have shown up downriver, on a bank, providing the boys were killed on impact and couldn't get the car out of the river. I don't know, that's why I want to have my own look."

We got our hiking gear together and loaded the car. Spirit took up his customary seat in the back. He seemed to sense there was a shift in the paradigm. We never spoke of "the kiss" again.

As we neared the supposed point where Chuck's car ran off the road, we peered from the car windows deep into the forested land that went on for acres and acres, miles and miles. The trees crawled up the mountainsides and back down again. There were hidden clearings and sometimes the undergrowth was so dense it was like looking into midnight.

"Me thinks this will not be an easy trek," Wally observed taking in the tangle of vines and scrub brush.

Now to find a place to park, hopefully out of direct sight. I was still looking over my shoulder expecting to see Lydia Jackson barreling straight at me on her broom.

We got out of the car, adjusted our backpacks, and let Spirit run into the woods to take care of business. There was a lot of wildlife in these wildlands. Black bear, elk, wolves, cougars, all manner of four-legged beasts that saw us as prime rib. I always thought it was odd I was never afraid when roaming these mountains. There was such a strong connection to my soul, it never occurred to me to be afraid. Oh, snakes. Did I mention our charming array of copperheads, timber rattlers, and water moccasins? I didn't? That must have been a Freudian slip. Luckily, it was still cold enough the bears were still in their dens and the snakes…well, wherever snakes went when it got too cold for them.

"Where to?" Wally broke through my mental meanderings.

"I guess we just dive headfirst into the thicket," I suggested.

Thankfully the thicket was no more than a temper tantrum as we tumbled out into, not a clearing, per se, but at least we could see more than the leaves of brambles and feel the whip of a sapling limb in our face. If anyone ever tells you the forest is cool and refreshing, quiet and serene, I'm here to tell you they're lying. It was noisy, and cold and snow rained on us as the sun melted the top canopy. Woodpeckers were banging on the trees in search of tasty bugs, birds scratching in the leaves, water flowing in rivers covered with rhododendrons, some animal making grunting noises, feet running down a hidden path and crows screaming at each other. I could barely hear myself think!

"Maybe we're looking in the wrong direction," Wally suggested.

Really? Ya think? I thought. "And what direction should we be looking? I mean, if the car was disabled, it couldn't have gotten too far. Even if it wasn't disabled, look how thick the vegetation is in here. Unless they were driving a bulldozer, I doubt they could maneuver through all this."

"That is true. That being said, how much longer do you want to look? I'm getting hungry," he said.

"I think we've pretty well covered this area. Let's think about other possibilities and come back. I'm hungry too," I agreed, realizing I had forfeited breakfast in favor of a crying jag.

We headed back to the car. "Spirit! Come, come!" I called.

The crows continued to fuss at each other, a squirrel in the tree next to us started lobbing acorns, but no Spirit. Okay, don't panic. "Spirit!"

Out of the corner of my eye, I saw something dark run among the trees. "Spirit! Come, come!" I yelled. The shadow didn't look like Spirit, actually. To be honest, it didn't look like a shadow, it was just so fast, it was a blur. A bear?

All of a sudden, I felt claustrophobic, the noise deafening, the foliage closing in on us. I needed to get out of here! My mouth, my throat, my nose felt it was filling with hot water. I swallowed and coughed trying to clear it. My skin became cold and clammy. My head swimming as I fought for air. I felt myself clawing at my throat, reaching for some unseen thing. Then, there was nothing. I looked at Wally. He was looking into the woods. He hadn't noticed anything at all. I felt weak and confused. I felt as if I was dying, and he noticed nothing.

"I think I see him coming," he said turning to me. "Red? Are you okay?"

I felt a little disoriented. "I think the cold is getting to me," I brushed it off.

"You look like you went swimming! And you're as pale as a...well, I was going to say ghost, but apparently, ghosts aren't always white. You sure you're okay? Drink some of your water and let's rest just a minute."

As much as I wanted to get out of there, I sat on the first available fallen tree. My legs felt shaky and my lungs hurt. If I had a wild imagination, I would think I just relived the drowning of Chuck and his friends. If I had a wild imagination. More likely, I was dehydrated as Wally surmised. I drank the water and soon, Spirit came bounding out of the thicket. His noble face wearing that goofy wolf grin.

"Let's go. I'm ready for some heat and quiet," I said, standing and heading back to the car. Just one problem though. Where was the car?

Chapter Twenty-Eight

We had no way of knowing just how far we had wandered off. We went in circles more than once. Nothing looked familiar, everything looked familiar. I felt a tickle in my stomach as I realized we were lost.

"We'll find our way," I said to reassure Wally, and myself.

"Of course, we will," he agreed.

We hacked at bushes, pushed back limbs, stepped over logs, and walked and walked and walked. I was getting frustrated, Wally was getting tired, and Spirit was having a blast. The sun moved across the sky and the shadows started getting darker and longer across the forest floor. I couldn't help but think of that dark shape that seemed to be stalking us. I did not want to be trapped in here at night.

We rested again, against my silent protest. I didn't want to waste valuable daylight hours.

"We should be getting close," Wally took a swig of water, shaking the last drop from the bottle.

"I don't think so," I admitted, "I think we should accept the fact that we're lost."

"No. No, we aren't lost. We just haven't found the right path to take yet," he tried to sound upbeat. I could tell he was also worried and frustrated and hungry and tired.

He laughed and called Spirit. Spirit ran to him sitting in front of him with bright eyes and a tongue hanging out. "Spirit, can you take us to the car?"

"Oh, that's sure to work. We're saved," I said, sarcasm dripping from my voice.

"Well, why not? This is his world," Wally defended himself.

I looked around, stood up and surveyed the endless trees that were getting darker by the minute, "Nope. I don't think so. I don't see my bed anywhere, and where are the food dishes with fresh meat and clean water?"

"You're tired and cranky," Wally said, not helping the situation at all.

I sat back down and sighed. "I guess we just start walking again. Don't you know how to plot a course with the moon and stars and stuff? Were you never a boy scout?"

Wally just shook his head. Spirit looked from one to the other. I'm sure he was wondering why these two humans were together when all they did was argue and fight. Truth be told, I suppose that was our language of love. Some people get all lovey-dovey, we just argue.

I picked up my backpack and began to walk. Wally and Spirit quickly joined.

"Where are we going?" Wally asked,

On the verge of tears of frustration, I hacked my way through the undergrowth, "Somewhere, anywhere, at least I'm not sitting like a prime rib on a platter!"

I saw the look Spirit and Wally gave each other. I just didn't care. We walked until it got too dark to see any further. Wally began gathering sticks and wood. He piled it in a small pile. He stuffed leaves among the wood and then pulled a lighter out of his pocket and lit the wood. Soon there was a comforting fire. We didn't let it get too big for fear of setting the canopy afire above us, but we sat watching the flames.

As I sat letting my dark mood come out to play, something fluttered by my ear. Another damned bug! I swatted it. A few seconds later, another. Annoyed I swatted it too and got up to move closer to the fire. I saw Wally swat at something too, but it sure didn't look like a bug!

Breathlessly, I motioned to get Wally's attention.

"What?"

"Wally, look!" I pointed to the next 'bug'.

We watched as a hundred-dollar bill floated from the tree and down to where we were seated.

"What the hell?" Wally said, bewildered.

"It's money!" I exclaimed, stating the obvious.

"I know it's money, genius, but from where?" he asked, peering into the black canopy of the trees.

"It's too dark to see," I said, again, stating the obvious.

"Great deduction, Sherlock," Wally groused.

"Okay. I vote we stay right here tonight and, in the morning, do a little investigating," I said gathering up the stray bills that didn't go right into the fire.

Wally began to pick up the currency as well. We stuffed the money in my backpack and when we couldn't find any more within the illumination of the fire, we sat on the logs once again and waited until morning. I don't know what Wally was thinking about, but I was praying we didn't get attacked by a bear or a mountain lion while we waited for daybreak.

All of a sudden, I jerked awake. The birds were chattering non-stop, snow dripped from the leaves onto my head. The forest had turned into a misty, foggy gray. It looked pretty eerie; I have to say. I wondered at first if this was one of those weird dreams, I was prone to having these days. I tried to get my saliva glands to work, but they were as dry as my throat.

Just out of our little circle, I saw frozen wild elderberries the critters had somehow missed. I plucked some from the arched branches and popped them in my mouth. Super sweet and very juicy, I began to feel better. I filled my hand with the sweet berries and went to Wally, who was sprawled out on the ground by his log.

"Hey, wake up!" I hissed. I poked him a bit and his eyes slowly opened. I poked him again.

"Geez, Red, stop poking me!" he groused.

"Look! Elderberries! They're delicious!" I said popping another in my mouth.

Wally was suddenly alert and hungrily took the offered berries, cramming all of them in his mouth. His eyes closed in appreciation for the sweet, juicy syrup flowing down his throat. He joined me at the bushes, and we ate our fill.

"Oh, my gosh, I needed that!" he exclaimed.

"Me too!" I agreed.

He stood and looked up into the tree. At first, we couldn't see anything. Then as the sun broke through the mist, we could see something dull. We circled the tree still looking up.

"Wait! I see something!" he shouted, pointing straight up.

I went to his side of the tree and shaded my eyes. "I think I see it too!"

The sunlight became brighter and there, in the upper branches of the tree, was the silhouette of a car. A 1954 Cadillac, to be exact!

"How the *HELL* did it get way up there?" Wally asked in amazement.

"Do you think that's it?" I was breathless.

Wally looked at me, "Oh, I don't know, Red. I would imagine there are hundreds of 1954 Cadillacs hanging out in the tops of trees all over these mountains."

"Smartass," I said under my breath.

"The question we should be asking is, how are we going to get it down?" I said. "Do you think those boys are still in it?"

Wally looked at me like I had grown two heads. "That's gross and I didn't even think of that. Their families are gonna want to finally lay them to rest. We're going to need help, Red. There's no way we can get a car down that's been stuck up in a tree for forty years."

"One of us could climb up there and try to dislodge it," I suggested.

Three sets of eyes traveled up at least twenty-five feet up the limbless tree trunk.

"I don't think so," Wally said slowly.

"What if I hoisted you up as far as possible and you skootched the rest of the way?" I suggested.

"Skootch? Me? Why me?" Wally protested.

"Because you're the guy!" I answered.

"What does *that* mean?" still protesting, I see.

"I don't know, aren't guys supposed to do the heroic thing?"

"Yeah, no, I don't see that happening," he said with disgust.

"Okay. Then how about we find a big limb from a tree and try to poke it down?" I tried another approach.

"Red, you really don't understand physics at all, do you? If we found a limb that big, can you even imagine how heavy it would be? Even with two of us, we wouldn't be able to stabilize it enough to get a two-thousand-pound car to move."

"Well, Mr. Know-It-All, what bright suggestions do you have?" I was thoroughly irritated with Wally and seriously starting to question his rights to a man card.

"Red, I don't think we have a choice, we're going to have to call for help," he said those dreaded words.

"No! I mean, not yet. Wally, if people come help, Rosa's money is as good as gone and we'll never be able to help Peter find peace."

We both whirled around when we heard heavy steps kicking up leaves. Every once in a while, we could hear a cuss word, but it was too muted to tell who it might be. We stood stock-still, hoping they would just bypass us and not try to investigate why a man, a woman, and a wolf stood looking up a tree. The noise got louder. Whoever it was certainly didn't mind making noise.

From the thicket, out popped Aunt Jo! She looked up and saw us.

"Oh, for crying out loud, Probably! In the middle of the woods? Really?" she spat out a bit of dirt and removed leaves from her hair. Her long skirt was tied between her legs and her aviator hat was askew. Then she turned her gaze upon us and let me tell you, she did not look happy. She spat again and swiped her hair out of her face. She was glaring at me.

Chapter Twenty-Nine

"**A**unt Jo! What are you doing here? How did you find us? Thank God, you found us!" I ran up to her and gave her a hug. She accepted it stiffly and sniffed.

Wally was still trying to get on her good side, so he pointed at the tree, "Look! I think we found it!"

Aunt Jo took the glare off me and centered Wally in her crosshairs. "Young man, 'it' covers a lot of territory. If you have something to say, please, be specific."

"Aunt Jo, we found the Cadillac!" I said trying to rescue Wally.

That got Aunt Jo's attention. "Ohhhh," she said drawing out the word. Wally and I pointed up into the tree. Aunt Jo shielded her eyes from the sun and peered into the network and tangled limbs of the canopy. "How'd it get way up there?"

"It doesn't really matter at this point. What we're trying to figure out, is how to get it down," I said, feeling the excitement drain away into hopelessness.

"Well, that certainly is a conundrum," she agreed, "But that's your problem, not mine. I'm still trying to figure out why Vera sent me out here in the armpit of hell."

"Maybe because she wanted you to show us how to get home?" I offered.

"Pffft," she huffed, "I'm your protector, not your tour guide."

Wally smiled as he realized where Probably got that interminable spunk. Talk about two birds of a feather.

Spirit stood, shoulders tensed, hackles up. He emitted a low growl deep in his throat. I felt my stomach clench. The shadow that followed us all day yesterday, it must have been Brendore hoping we would lead him to the money. Which we did. Stupid, stupid, stupid.

Aunt Jo lifted her head and closed her eyes. "There is more than one this time. And they are angry! Probably, RUN!"

At that exact moment she was lifted off the ground and slammed into a tree! I watched horrified. Running was not an option, peeing my pants was. Wally yelled something and all at once, there were dark shadows all around us. We stood back to back watching the demons surround us. They were snarling as they took shape from shadow to demon and advanced on us. Spirit was tensed and ready to spring into action. I chanced a look at my aunt, she was out cold, if not dead. We heard more scuffling in the leaves. What new hell is upon us now?

Lydia Jackson emerged from the thicket, unscathed, but what I saw next made my blood run cold. There stood Rocco with a smug look on his face.

"We'll be taking what's ours now," she said.

"Over my dead body," I said without thinking, then I thought that might be a self-fulfilling prophesy, "Or let me rephrase that."

Lydia laughed and it was pure evil. "I knew it was only a matter of time before you couldn't keep your nose out of other people's business. You just couldn't resist having the money to yourself."

I tried to steel myself, but I felt like I was made of Jell-O. "What was your connection to the money? Peter wanted Rosa and their child to have it. That's what I aim to do, give it to the ones who really have a claim to it."

"Oh, listen to you, all noble like. Honey, you won't even make it out of these woods alive."

The creatures restlessly tightened the circle. Wally grabbed my hand and held on tight.

"Rocco is the connection," Wally whispered.

"She's not alive, Red, remember the real Lydia Jackson died many years ago? Aunt Jo tried to tell us."

It dawned on me. Yes, she did try to tell me and as usual, I brushed it off as an old woman and a bad memory. That meant, Lydia was a demon, *the* demon.

"Brendore!" I shouted. "What demon hides in an old woman?" I saw her cock her head. "WOW! I'm scared! Can you see me shaking?" As an added insult, I laughed.

I saw the demon begin to transition.

"Are you freakin' out of your mind?" Wally hissed. "You're pissing her off, Red!"

"Oh, Brendore? I have a question. Do we fight with walkers or with canes?" I laughed even harder. It was having the desired effect, she was trembling and changing into something I couldn't even place in a nightmare. I am not so stupid as to tell you, that I wasn't afraid. I have never been so terrified in my life, but the only answer was to defeat this undead army.

"GIVE ME THE MONEY, NOW!" she roared.

"What the hell you gonna do with money?" I shouted back at her. "You guys got a Demon General over there on your side? Or did Little Rocky introduce you to a worthy cause? At any rate, you're getting nothing from me."

Out of the corner of my eye, I saw Aunt Jo stir. Very discreetly she gave me a thumbs up.

Brendore grew to twelve feet tall, with great horns curling from his head, his sharp, pointed teeth snapping in uncontrolled rage. He ripped up trees and threw them as though they were nothing more than toothpicks.

"You die!" He screamed, and his demon army converged upon us. Sparks flew throughout the forest surrounding us. I grabbed a tree limb from the ground and swung wildly hoping to connect and disable the closest demon. Their sharp claws emitted fire; their rank smell turned my stomach. A spark glanced off my cheek and I could immediately feel the sting of a burn. It wasn't a hot burn, it felt more like cauterized flesh. I saw Wally parrying his own tree limb.

"Don't let them touch you!" I screamed at him.

Dried wood and leaves caught fire. A demon grabbed Wally and I heard that idiot laugh, "Here we go again!"

I tried to fight them off as best I could. I thought back to all those supernatural movies I'd seen as a kid, and this was nothing like that. I was dodging fireballs, jumping behind trees for cover, and desperately looking for something, anything stronger I could use as a weapon. Brendore managed to get me separated from my 'tribe'. Saliva dripped from his gaping jaws. He smelled really bad.

"Give me the money," he growled.

"Get a breath mint," I countered.

He started to reach for me, then pulled back.

We both stopped as we heard an unholy howl come from deep within the forest. It was answered by more howls. It was something I always imagined a banshee would sound like. Brendore swung his head toward the sound and I used the momentary distraction to pick up a rock and throw it at him, aiming for his head, but, of course, landing somewhere in his midsection. Well, that just infuriated him more.

He grabbed me by the hair and yanked me off my feet. The air left my lungs as he swung me high above the ground. I could see the tree coming straight at me. This would kill me. I took a breath and searched for Wally. He lay against a tumble of boulders, motionless. The impact was imminent, and I would be dead. My last thought was, *geez, I really suck at fighting demons.*

The impact never came. I opened one eye, then the other. There was a comforting blue glow around me. I heard Brendore roaring in anger, demons screaming, growls, yelps, but it all sounded like I was underwater. They were just sounds. I saw hundreds of wolves attacking the army and Brendore frantically trying to fend them off. Brendore was changing from demon to Lydia Jackson like static on a TV. Wally was sitting now, encased by the blue glow. I could do nothing but observe, as I lazily floated head over heel among the upper branches of the trees. I guess I passed out, or maybe my brain had seen all it could handle and shut down.

The last thing I remember seeing, the demons were fleeing back into the woods and Brendore turning back into a shadow, which disappeared like smoke.

It seemed so silent. No birds singing, no squirrels chattering, no leaves rustling. It was as though all sound left with the demons.

"Where's Red?" I heard Wally shout.

"Up here!" I called back waving from the treetop.

"What are you doing up there? How'd you get up there?" he yelled, shading his eyes to see me better.

"Hell, if I know!" I scooted to a more comfortable spot.

Aunt Jo didn't look so good. She slumped against the tree and hung her head. Ever so slowly, she slid down the trunk and collapsed on the ground.

Wally ran to her and lifted her in his arms, "Jo!" he said shaking her gently. "Jo! You're going to be okay. Red! Help her!"

I looked at my current situation and my eye spied something directly below me. A 1954 Cadillac convertible! However, though I was close to the trunk of the car, there were no branches to help me down out of this precarious perch.

Aunt Jo began to rouse a little. Wally was stroking her forehead, tenderly tucking her stray hair away from her face. She was awfully white; I could see that even from my vantage point. "She okay?" I shouted.

"I'm not sure," Wally shouted back.

"I'm okay. Where's my damned hat?" I heard her say, though it sounded like a mumble.

"She's okay!" Wally shouted.

"Would you please stop that infernal shouting!" she groused as she struggled to sit up. She began to crawl on the ground looking for her aviator hat. When she found it, she plopped it on her head, stood, and brushed the mud and snow from her skirts.

"I found the car!" I called down.

"We found the car before we got attacked!" Wally called back, eyeing Aunt Jo to see if he was going to get yelled at again for shouting.

"No! I mean, I'm practically sitting on it! Has anyone seen Spirit?"

Wally and Aunt Jo looked at each other and shook their heads. They immediately began to search for him. I could do no more than sit in this damned tree and try to figure out how to get down, or more importantly, how to get the car down. I kept glancing at my two friends, looking for Spirit. I hoped he was okay; I don't know what I'd do if anything happened to him. Rather than sit and worry, when there was nothing I could do to contribute on the ground, I tried to reason a way to get out of this predicament.

This far up in the trees, most of the snow had melted and a thin layer of ice coated the bark. The trunk of the car was pointing down. That made it even more difficult. It was lodged in the fork of some branches. That's why it was so hard to see. To the casual observer, the years of accumulated rust looked like more tree trunk.

I stuck my toe out and tested the holding potential. For the first time, I was really grateful for my long legs. Whether they were long enough or not, remained to be determined. I stretched my leg out and found a footing on a lower branch, slipping a little on the ice. I could only hope it was strong enough to hold me. I eased down, holding on to the tree like a monkey.

Finally, I reached the branch and gave a timid little bounce. Okay. So far, so good. I gently lowered myself to a sitting position and looked at the next branch. It was a little closer with lots of little limbs sticking out of it like spines. I stretched my leg out to it and found footing right away. The fork of the branch looked sturdy, so I scooted over to the fork and wiggled my butt into a more secure position. I could feel the wet cold seeping through the seat of my jeans.

The car was still about three branches away. I hugged the branch and gently rolled off it and found myself hanging in empty air. I forgot to gauge the distance of the next branch or the size of it. So, there I was, hanging like a sheet on a clothesline, not sure what to do. My shoulders were screaming in protest. I was going to have to think of something quick. It's not like I was a member of a gym and used to hanging several feet from the ground from a branch and unforgiving ground below. I hung there, trying to decide what to do.

Karma took care of it, no worries. My hands began to lose control on the ice, then slide, then released the branch. I could feel myself falling, the rough bark scraping my chin and cheek. It hurt. It really, really hurt! I came to rest on the next branch in an undignified heap, knocking the breath out of me. Cheek and chin burning like fire, my back feeling like it was broken, I gingerly sat on the small branch, as close to the main trunk as possible. I sat trying to pull air into my lungs and resisting the urge to check my wounds. I was sweating like a turkey the day before Thanksgiving.

I had to sit. I had no choice. In a minute, I'd try for the next one. Only two more to go. I felt weak before I remembered I hadn't eaten since our trail mix the afternoon before. Thirsty and hungry, I began to have thoughts that we just may not get out of this alive. My back was throbbing. I needed to quit fiddle-farting around and get serious about getting out of this tree. I quickly glanced at movement on the ground and saw Wally and Aunt Jo return to the war zone. I bounced a little on the branch and all at once, it broke, and I felt myself free-falling from the top of the tree.

Chapter Thirty

While it is not unheard of, it *is* rare, many people do not experience their death. Say, for example, they're in a vehicle accident and killed instantly. One minute you're enjoying the blue sky and the sun on your face, the next you're shaking hands with Peter Euclid. Most diseases end during a coma, you're here, then you're there. I was one of the 'not unheard of's', I was experiencing every painful step to death's door. I felt the skin peel from my body, the stick that speared my kidney, the instant headache when my head bashed against the tree. I landed on my mid-section on a branch and felt the wind knocked out of me with a mighty *Umph!* and my pelvic bones ground to dust. Did I stop my tumble into oblivion? Nope. I continued my downward journey. I was pretty sure this was the end.

All at once I smacked into something hard. I dared open my eyes and found myself sprawled over the hood of the Cadillac. The car frame rocked, and I rolled through the broken out windshield frame, landing on the gear shifter, and into the laps of two skeletons. I looked into the empty eye sockets and the toothy grins of naked mandibles. Well, I found the boys.

I peeked over the side and saw Aunt Jo and Wally gazing up in horrified terror, their eyes as wide as their open mouths.

I peeked over the side, gave them a thumbs-up, and shouted, "I'm okay!" Then I fell back into the laps of my heroes thinking, *I'm dying*. I gasped for breath, a sweat broke out and ran into my eyes and down my nose. I tried to take a cursory inventory but, apparently, there was not one square inch that wasn't screaming in pain.

Instinct told me, the longer I laid there, the harder it would be to finish my mission. Sorry, Death, not today! I crawled over the seat and surveyed the trunk. It was partially open, which accounted for our rain of money the night before. I figured the branches had to be pretty strong to hold this car for forty-five years, so I chanced crawling out on one. My knees burned like fire and my arm refused to obey. I held it close to my side when I could and resisted the urge to scream in agony when I couldn't. I could see the car was not only wedged, but the tree was starting to grow around it. The fork in the branches was pretty solid from what I could see.

I looked down at my audience, who had not moved a muscle. "I think I can get to the trunk!" I yelled.

I straddled the branch and scooted to the trunk area. There was no way I was going to get that trunk open. I took a chance and positioned myself so I could kick it with my feet. I could hear rust and brittle metal filter down into the interior. I kicked again with my feet and this time; they went all the way through. Okay, trunk is now open. How to get down in there and get the money, providing it was still there. I leaned over as far as I could to see what I could see. It was dark, for sure, but I could barely make out a couple of duffle bags and a rotted, wooden chest.

I sat back and weighed my options. I could take a chance and slide down into the trunk or...okay, I had one option. Taking a breath that nearly sent me screaming in pain, I slid down into the trunk. The car rocked and I heard weak metal protest. The car may not fall, but it could break into pieces and take me with it. I quickly threw the duffle bags out of the car. I looked at the wooden chest. The wood was rotted, and larvae had taken up residence. All at once a squirrel shot out of the car and scampered along the branch, cussing me up one side and down the other. I instinctively ducked and when I did, the floorboard of the trunk gave way and down went the chest, with money fluttering like dried leaves.

Problem solved. Now, to figure out how to get out of here myself. I hoisted myself back to the branch and just sat looking around. I swatted away a vine that insisted on tangling itself in my hair. My scalp was plenty sore from the yanking it got from Brendore, so no, I didn't want anything touching me. Finally, I yanked on the vine to rip it from its moorings and be done with it, when I realized just how strong it was! I wondered...

Having only one good arm, I wrapped the vine around my good wrist and wound my legs around the free-swinging part. Here goes! It will either be the answer or the journey into death's hollows would be completed. Painfully, inch by excruciating inch, I allowed the vine to thread through my hand and used my legs to stabilize me. After what seemed like an eternity, I felt hands grab me and ease me back to solid ground. I lay back in the decaying leaves and rotting debris and just counted my blessings. As I lay there, a torrent of acorns battered my head and face. Apparently, Mr. Squirrel had his nest in the old car, and I had disturbed it. Know what? I hurt so bad and was so grateful to be on the ground again, I didn't even move.

Wally was kneeling beside me. "Oh my God, Red! I thought you were a goner!" He was examining me. "I think you may have broken your arm, does it hurt to breathe? I don't know where to look first!"

Aunt Jo watched us and produced a flask from her skirt. Thank God, I could use a bit of painkiller. Instead, she took a long pull, and looked at me, wiping her mouth.

"You gonna be able to walk outta here?"

Wally shot her a glance. "Red, Spirit's hurt real bad. He needs help."

That brought me around better than anything alcohol could have. "What? Where is he?"

"He's over there. He's been laying there since we put him there. We need to get him to that vet as soon as possible," Wally said. When he looked over at the large wolf laying so still, I could see tears in his eyes. Heck, there were tears in mine too.

Even though I hurt with every movement, large or small, I told Wally we needed to make a litter and we'd have to pull him through the woods.

"We don't know where we are though," Wally reminded me. "We could walk for days!"

"Oh, for crying out loud. Follow me!" Aunt Jo grumbled.

We made a hurried sled to load Spirit on and Aunt Jo led the way. We pulled Spirit on the makeshift litter made of saplings and vines still young enough to be broken. It was a struggle. It hurt to take a breath, so my breathing was shallow, which made me dizzy. Still, I refused to give up. Spirit needed me.

I heard the brave wolf whisper, "Thank you."

That did it. I pulled, panted, and cried, desperately praying that we would be in time to save him.

Though in reality, it wasn't all that far, my battered and broken body felt like we walked forever. Spirit had closed his eyes in spite of the jostling and rough ground. Every step was agony, both physically and emotionally. However, eventually, we arrived at the road. There sat our glorious, wonderful, heaven-sent car! Aunt Jo buckled her aviator cap and put on yellow goggles. She hoisted herself on a small red scooter and putt-putted away down the road. She was a little bit wobbly, but no wonder, I'm sure that flask was nearly empty at this point.

Wally and I struggled with a yelp escaping me when I thoughtlessly used my injured arm.

"We need to get you to the hospital. I'm pretty sure that arm is broken," Wally said as he lifted most of Spirit's weight into the back seat of the car. I pretended to help with my right arm. We loaded the duffel bags into the trunk, along with our backpacks stuffed full of money from the wooden chest.

"No hospitals!" I was adamant. If we went to the hospital, they would want details. We could make something up, but I hurt too bad to be that creative. By the time we were seated, Wally in the passenger seat, me behind the steering wheel, I was beyond exhausted. I couldn't even see clearly, no doubt along with everything else, I most likely could add concussion to my whining rights.

"Want me to drive?" Wally asked.

"No. I'm good," I said stubbornly. The problem was, I couldn't remember how to start the car! I just sat there staring at the dash, hoping for enlightenment.

"Move over. I'm driving, Red. I'm sure you're fine, but I don't want to get killed in a car, after nearly being killed by the Underworld Overlord. Kind of anti-climactic, don't you think?"

I wanted to protest, I really did, but instead, I got out of the car and crossed over to the passenger side. Wally remembered how to start the car and I hated him for it.

Our first stop was the animal care clinic where the vet, Mary Quanko, who first saw Spirit when he was a pup, worked. She had her assistants come out to the car and carry him into the exam room. She gently poked and prodded and when she got to his mid-section, he let out a little whimper. He looked at me as if to say, *I'm sorry. I'm trying to be brave.* I bent down and kissed the top of his head and told him it was alright. I let out a whimper too. Bending over was not a good idea. My rib cage was aching in time with my heartbeat and my back felt like it was broken. I observed that my ribcage and back hurt a lot worse than the arm.

"Are you okay?" Dr. Quanko asked.

"Sure, I'm fine. How's Spirit? Is he going to be okay?"

Mary pursed her lips and continued her exam. "Well, it appears he may have a broken rib. I'll want to do an x-ray to determine the extent of the injury. And I found these burns under his neck. Any idea how that may have happened?"

Try as I might, I just couldn't come up with a plausible, believable lie. "It's complicated," I hedged. Meanwhile, in my head, I was chanting, *Please, don't ask. Please, don't ask. Please, don't ask.*

After a stare down, she said she was taking Spirit back for x-rays and draw some blood to make sure there wasn't an infection setting in. Wally and I sat in the waiting room. I leaned my head against the wall and immediately fell asleep. I woke myself up with a snort when my head bobbed forward. Wally put his arm around me and pulled me into him, laying my head on his shoulder. I fell asleep again.

I woke again to someone touching my arm. I let out an involuntary yelp. In my blurry, half-asleep state, I'd forgotten where I was. A man was standing over me.

"Red, we need to get you to the hospital," he said softly.

"No! No hospitals!" I cried weakly.

The man straightened up and conferred with Dr. Quanko. "Red, I need you to hear me. Can you wake up enough to talk to me?"

My head did something similar to a nod. It actually felt like a balloon on a string, just kind of bobbing in the wind. Then, the fog began to lift ever so slightly. I smiled.

"Hi, Aaron," I mumbled.

"Hey, yourself. Red, I need you to listen to me. Dr. Quanko is going to take you back to the exam room and do some x-rays. We don't have to tell anyone. Okay? Can you give us permission to do that?"

Again, the balloon in the wind bobbed and bounced. Wally looked relieved.

I really don't remember too much after that. All that plays through my mind are the screams of pain as the veterinarian set my broken arm and taped up my ribs. I could hear them talking with Wally, but my brain was on vacation and I couldn't make heads or tails out of it.

"How's Spirit?" I whispered.

"He's going to be okay. I've taped up his ribs too and put him on some antibiotics," she said. "You two are going to have to recoup together."

I smiled like a drunk sailor being offered a free drink.

"How's Wally? He got thrown against some rocks," I said through waves of blurry comprehension.

I didn't see the look pass between the two, but I did hear Aaron say, "Don't ask questions. Let's just get her and Spirit home."

Wally came into the treatment room. Dr. Quanko told him I had asked about his back.

"Oh, heck, I'm fine," he said brushing it off.

"Let's take a look anyway, okay?" the vet insisted. She stopped when she saw the burn marks on Wally's jacket. No doubt when those *things* grabbed him to throw him against the tree.

I heard her sharp intake of breath. She shook her head and commented on his back, "You have some really deep bruising, Mr. Jenkins. I am concerned about blood clots. I can't write a prescription for that, not for humans, so I want you to promise to take two aspirin every day. One in the morning and one at night. It's important that you do that."

"I will. Thank you," Wally promised.

"If you experience any unfamiliar pain or swelling, it is imperative you follow up with your family doctor. Do you understand what I'm telling you?" she said staring him straight in the eye.

Wally nodded.

She turned and looked at Aaron, "They both should be in the emergency room."

Aaron agreed, but he reiterated he wouldn't go against my wishes.

The next cohesive moment found me in my own bed. Dr. Quanko kept Spirit overnight for observation and to keep him sedated until that rib could begin to heal. I turned and came face to face with Wally. His eyes were closed, and he was softly snoring. I positioned myself so I could spoon with him. He put an arm around me, and my breath hitched as pain tore

231

through my chest. It was worth it though. I closed my eyes and went back to sleep. I felt better having him there with me.

Chapter Thirty-One

The next two weeks were very quiet, maybe too quiet, or maybe not all that quiet, now that I look back on it. Things were happening. Things that seemed unconnected, but in retrospect, stringing them all together, something was happening alright.

First of all, not long after our battle in the mountains, Aunt Jo was hit by a pickup truck while riding her little red scooter. She wasn't hurt badly, but she was banged up pretty good. As they stood there fighting over whose fault it was, later investigation showed a glitch in the traffic light timing switch, which gave them both a green light. Though I grudgingly worried about her, I couldn't help but wish I'd been there to see her arguing with some poor soul who had no idea just who he was dealing with. It happens. I have a feeling the aviator hat saved her from a tragic injury.

Secondly, Miss Vera was out cleaning her flower beds to get them ready for spring. Beautiful day, no wind, no clouds, just a perfect day for outdoor gardening. Suddenly, a large limb from an apple tree came crashing down missing her by mere inches. As we looked at the errant branch, we saw it had rotted next to the joint. Okay, that happens freakishly rare, but it does happen.

Third, Bear Creek Elementary School caught fire. They managed to get all the children out in time, and thankfully there were no injuries, but still... The fire department released a statement that stated the cause of the fire was a faulty furnace switch. Uh-huh.

The fourth incident was the one that made me kind of reconsider these incidents were just random that's-life incidents. The fourth was when Wally went into town to buy groceries. I was still hobbling around, and he was wonderful at taking up the slack.

He walked into the grocery store and noticed it was very quiet and nearly empty. It was early afternoon and usually, there were people pushing carts, kids screaming, scanners *booping* as the cashier passed an item over it but it wasn't a law of science or anything and he just figured he lucked into the slow part of the day.

He noticed a young man standing in the back by the beer cooler. He seemed very intently studying the array of beers, but Wally noticed him watching him in the reflection of the glass. He decided to cut his shopping trip short and get the hell out of there! When he got to the checkout though, he noticed the cashier was shaking. Her eyes were full of fear. Wally said he felt the hairs on the back of his neck stand to attention.

"Do you need me to call the cops?" he whispered.

Her eyes darted away, and she nodded her head.

He said he had just pulled his wallet out to pay her when he felt a pressure in his back.

"May as well just hand me the money, man, I'm gonna take it anyway and whatever else you got in there," came a raspy voice.

Wally started to turn around and the gun jabbed him harder.

"Don't turn around. Just lay your wallet on the counter. Lady, you might as well go ahead and open that drawer," he commanded.

She punched some buttons and the drawer popped open. He instructed her to take ALL the money and lay it on the counter along with Wally's. She did. With one hand, he scooped up the money and jammed it in his hoodie pockets. He backed away and kind of side skipped to the door. Wally said he felt relief that all he lost was his money. The man stopped at the doors and turned back to them. He raised his gun and fired. *Pop! Pop! Pop!*

Then he ran out and disappeared down the sidewalk. The cashier fell onto the conveyor belt and Wally collapsed to the floor. He barely had the presence of mind to call 9-1-1. The police and fire department and an ambulance came screeching into the parking lot.

The cashier was already dead, her face laying in a pool of blood that dripped and flowed down the sides of the belt. Wally sustained a gunshot wound to the shoulder. They transported him to the hospital.

I got the call while I was listening to classical music, putting some ears of sweet corn on to boil for our BBQ ribs that night.

I still couldn't drive, so I limped to Miss Vera and she drove me to the hospital. Wally was feeling no pain as the doctors and nurses worked on him.

"Are you the one he keeps asking for?" the nurse asked as we entered the emergency exam room. "Are you Red?"

I nodded.

"We're getting ready to take him into surgery. The bullet is lodged near his spine. It entered his left shoulder and ricocheted off bone and settled next to his spinal column. He has you listed as next of kin," she said, all business.

"Hey, Red!" he called from his hospital bed. "Guess what? I got shot!"

The nurse rolled her eyes, "He's been going on about being beat up by demons and spooks and talking dogs. I swear. What kind of recreational drugs is he using?"

"What?" not sure I heard the question right.

"We need to know before we can do the surgery. There *is* the danger of drug interactions," she sniffed.

"Oh, right, yeah, of course."

"Well?"

"The only drug he takes is one aspirin in the morning and one aspirin at night...on doctor's orders. Although, I think he may have finished that prescription."

She didn't believe me, of that I'm certain.

I added to the story, "He has a wild imagination, that's why he's such a good writer."

"He's a writer? I'm an avid reader. What has he published?" she asked.

Caught off guard, I wasn't sure how to answer. She wasn't supposed to ask questions!

"Oh, you can just google Wallace Jenkins on Amazon," I lied. Please, don't look it up right now.

I was visibly relieved when a nurse came in to prep Wally for surgery. Poor Wally was snoring like a lumberjack. He roused a little and caught my eye.

"Hey, Red, I got shot!" he mumbled.

I could tell this was going to be a source of pride for him. I sent up a prayer that they would be able to fix him up good as new. Okay, I was worried. Happy now? They gave me his personal items to take home. The hospital didn't want the liability. I glanced through it, more as inventory than curiosity, but when I saw his phone, I hesitated. Should I call his parents?

They finished with him and wheeled him out of the room to take him into surgery. He was going in and out of consciousness, but he reached for my hand.

"Everything's going to be okay, buddy," I said with a definite huskiness to my voice.

"I have to tell you something," he held my hand tightly.

"Can it wait? They want to get you patched up."

"I love you," he whispered.

I stood there with my mouth hanging open. The nurse squeaked by me with a smirk on her face.

"Drugs," she said from the corner of her mouth.

I took a chair in the waiting room. There were other people waiting for word of their loved ones. I didn't want any conversation, so I took out my cell phone and stared at it. I'd been so busy that when the screen locked due to 'inactivity', I had no idea whatsoever how to turn it back on. So, I just sat there staring at a dark screen pretending to be totally engrossed.

A little girl of maybe six or seven-years-old sat in the chair next to me. I ignored her. I could feel her eyes on me. I shifted in my chair slightly turning my back to her. She just sat there staring.

"What?" I said irritably.

"Why you looking at nothing on your phone?" she asked.

"Because…because I don't…none of your business," I barked. No kid was going to show me up!

"You can play games on your phone," she suggested.

"No, I can't," I replied, "This phone doesn't come with games. It's a grown-up phone." Why did I have the urge to stick my tongue out at her?

"Don't you know how to turn your phone on?" Lord! Save me from this rugrat! An idea began to form. "I know how to work this phone, but you don't. It's way too complicated for a kid."

"I can so too work that phone! It's a piece of crap phone," she said as the insult hit home.

"Can not."

"Can so."

"Can not."

She grabbed the phone from my hand, "What's your PIN?"

"My what?" I asked.

"Your code!" the little snotty brat exclaimed as though I was an idiot.

"Corinthia! You give that lady back her phone and you watch your attitude, young lady!" her mother yelled from across the room.

Corinthia practically threw my phone at me, no doubt embarrassed by her mother.

"Hey, I like the name Corinthia," I said as a peace offering while mourning the fact that I came so close to finally getting my phone unlocked.

"You wanna know my name?" I asked.

Corinthia stared at me, crossed her arms and wrinkled her nose, "I already know. It's Skunk! You got those two white stripes in your hair. They look dumb!"

Mom came over and jerked her by the arm, dragging her across the waiting room floor. Only then did I notice the other families-in-waiting staring at me. They were shaking their heads and I'm not sure if they were shaking it at me or that little brat.

The nurse came into the room and called my name, I was happy for the escape. I nearly ran her over trying to get out of that room and away from snotty little girls.

Wally was going to be fine. They were able to retrieve the bullet, pump him full of antibiotics, and were just waiting for him to come out of recovery. I asked if I could see him, but she said I had to wait for at least two hours and even then, he would probably sleep most of the time.

There was no freakin' way I was going back into that waiting room, so I wandered the halls. I went into the cafeteria and ordered a tea and bag of chips. I sat at a table, alone, and watched birds fighting over crumbs on the outside patio. It was dim, quiet, and empty in the cavernous cafeteria. The whole atmosphere reeked of hopelessness and broken dreams.

"I want to apologize to you for Corinthia," a voice said at my elbow.

I looked up into the face of a relatively young mother. Her eyes spoke volumes, though her voice tried to sound brave, it was tinged with exhaustion.

I pushed back a chair and discreetly looked around for the tiny Hitler. "Oh, hey, no problem. Kids, huh? Please, have a seat for a minute, if you have time."

She smiled. "Corinthia is my wonder child," she began.

Yeah, wonder why you didn't keep your legs closed that night?

"You see, the day we brought her home from the hospital, a drunk driver ran the light and T-boned us on the driver's side. Her father was killed instantly. He didn't have a chance. Corrie was in her car seat, but that don't mean they prevent injury. She was hurt really bad. It was touch and go for a while. I didn't know if I'd be holding one funeral or two."

I felt awful for the thoughts I'd been having. I did something I've never done before; I reached over and laid my hand over hers. "I'm so sorry," I said, and I really meant it.

"Thank you. It's been rough these past six years. Corrie has some minimal brain damage. It causes inappropriate behavior sometimes," she explained.

"Oh, I think I may have provoked it somewhat," I confessed. "You see, I've never really been around kids. They're a mystery to me, but she seems like an extremely bright little girl!"

Mom smiled and nodded, "When it comes to technology, she's a genius! Anyway, I just wanted to apologize." She stood as though she lifted the weight of the world with her.

"I wish you both luck. I can't even imagine the weight you carry," I told her.

As I watched her walk out of the room, I saw a man follow her. He stopped at the door and turned to me. Her husband was still watching over his girls. He smiled.

"They're going to be okay, daddy," I whispered.

Chapter Thirty-Two

The nurse was right. Wally slept all afternoon, rousing only for a few minutes to let me know he'd been shot. I patted his hand and told him to go back to sleep. I kept picturing him holding my hand before he went in for surgery and whispering, *I love you*. The nurse was probably right about that as well...he was just feeling the melancholy of the sedatives. I promised myself I wouldn't read too much into it. That would be one ginormous elephant in the room if we spoke about it. Another ground rule, no elephants. Sure, we cared about each other, but a declaration of love?

I couldn't get Corinthia and her mom out of my mind. I kept seeing that bouncing, spitfire of a little girl, and her mother who only looked older because of her grief and fatigue. That was a love story right there. I pictured the husband standing beside his wife as she was told to push. He probably leaned over and kissed her with the screaming baby girl between them. They would tell each other *I love you* and then kiss the baby and say *I love you* again. The big day comes when they go home as a family. Bright expectations, excitement to finally have something other than stuffed toys in the crib, nervousness because they've never been a family before.

Then, in the blink of an eye, it vaporized amidst broken glass, twisted metal, and death. How could she go on? How much did she sleep while mourning the loss of her husband, and the desperate prayers to save their child?

The vision came back to haunt me as Miss Vera drove me home. I got ready for bed and lay on the floor with Spirit and cried. Spirit nuzzled me and shared my sorrow.

The next morning, I was in the kitchen fixing my hot tea when Aunt Jo came breezing in like a hurricane.

"Don't you ever fix coffee anymore?" she complained.

"No," was the short answer.

"You look like hell. How's the guy?" she asked as she sniffed my Earl Gray tea, wrinkling her nose.

"Thank you and he's going to be okay. He has a name, Aunt Jo. His name is Wally," I snapped.

"Yeah, Willy, Wally, whatever. You two sleeping together yet?"

"Aunt Jo!"

"What?" she asked with an innocence that didn't fool me one bit. "Good grief, if you don't want people jumping to conclusions, then don't live together."

"Did you want something in particular?" I shoved two pieces of toast in front of her.

"Oh, just wondering if you've learned anything new. It's been so quiet. Kind of got me nervous," she said between mouthfuls. "Brendore is no quitter."

I looked at her incredulous that she seemed oblivious to the past three weeks. "Gee, Aunt Jo, I've been a little busy fighting demons and nearly getting killed and Wally getting shot. I don't know where the time goes!"

She gave me a bored, but snotty look.

"Actually, Aunt Jo, there is something I want to talk to you about," I said, changing the subject.

She wiped the crumbs off her hands onto the floor and took a sip of her tea. I gave her a look of disapproval. "Don't worry. Spirit will clean it up. Now, shoot."

"I'm not sure if I'm just being paranoid or what, but I'm wondering at some of the things that have been happening lately," I began.

"Oh? Like what?" she asked.

"Well, you getting mowed down by that pickup truck, for starters."

"There was a glitch in the switch," then she laughed, "Get it? A glitch in the switch?"

I didn't laugh, no sense encouraging her. "And then that thing with Miss Vera. If we were having a storm I could understand, but a perfectly beautiful day?"

"Didn't you tell me that old branch was rotted?"

"Well, yeah, see, that's just it. Everything has a perfectly reasonable explanation, but it just doesn't feel right. The school burning. I think the one that hit home the most was Wally getting shot. That guy already had the money and anything else he wanted. He actually started to leave and then turned around and shot them!"

Aunt Jo was paying attention now.

"You think Brendore is behind all this?" she asked.

"You said he was no quitter. I feel like he's tightening the noose, so to speak. Hoping to disable anyone close to me that may help me," I reasoned.

"What about the school? How does that tie in?"

I thought about that, I'd been thinking about it. "The only thing I can figure is that Wally and I found out that Peter and Rosa did get together and produce a child. I think Brendore is letting us know, he knows about the child."

"Boy or girl?" she asked.

"We don't know at this point. Just that there was a child. We suspect Peter wants the money to go to that child or the descendant of that child."

Aunt Jo sat in deep thought. She went to the toaster and put two more slices of bread in. I'd never really seen her at a loss for words. It was kind of scary if you want me to be honest.

Finally, she sat back down, "I think you may be on to something. You know, people have some misconceptions about the other side. They think these ghosts just hang around and have no clue as to modern times. There is greed there, power struggles, they dabble in our politics, relationships, our day to day. They caused trouble when they were alive, and they cause trouble when they're dead. Brendore wants that money bad enough to kill for it."

I felt the hairs on my arm stand on end. "So, we're in danger too."

"Unless we figure out a resolution. Do you have the money here?"

I looked at her straight in the eye, "You'll forgive me if I don't answer that question."

She nodded.

I looked at the oven clock, "I need to get to the hospital. Wally will have finished breakfast now. I'll give him your love."

She snorted.

I was walking the hospital hallway to his room when I saw Corinthia and her mom sitting in the waiting room. I waved. The mom waved back, Corinthia just looked at me blankly. Oh, how soon the young forget.

I took a detour and went over and sat beside them.

"Hi!" I greeted her. "And there's Corinthia! Hey, I wondered if I could ask your help with something."

"What?" she asked giving me a look straight out of The Exorcist.

"Well, I really do have a problem with my phone," I began.

"Like what?"

"I don't know how to work it. Your mom says you know all about these things, so I thought I should ask an expert," I said amicably. In my mind, I remembered seeing the dad walk out with his wife. I could tell love endured the grip of death, just as strongly as evil held on to its victims.

"Like what?" she repeated.

"Well, for starters, how do you turn this danged thing on?" I laughed.

Corinthia rolled her eyes and shook her head. I offered her my phone. She took it and studied it for a minute.

"What's your password?"

"You know what? I don't have one. Can you help me with one?" I never felt so stupid as I did sitting in a hospital waiting room begging a six-year-old child to help me with a phone.

"Skunk. Your new password is Skunk," she said with a smirk.

"Corinthia!" her mother gasped.

I laughed, "No, it's okay. She's talking about the two white streaks in my hair, not my body odor. Right?"

"Whatever," she replied.

While her stubby child fingers flew across the screen of my phone and I saw the screen change from one format to another, I turned to her mother.

"We didn't get properly introduced yesterday," I reached into my pocket and pulled out my driver's license. "My name is Probably Magic Sarangoski. Here's my license so you can see that really is my name."

I saw her eyes dart to me and the license.

"That's a very unique name! I thought Corinthia was original, but I believe you've got that beat," she laughed.

"Corinthia is a beautiful name. How did she come by that?" I asked.

"Oh, our family is big on tradition. Corinthia is actually an old family name. We have a lot of skeletons in our family tree," she explained with a soft chuckle.

I nodded and returned a smile, "Mine too. I think that's the nature of family trees. Heck, if you shake my family tree, you'd be buried by the nuts falling out of it!"

She had a musical laugh and as she laughed, I could see some of the exhaustion and pain slip away.

"Want to compare notes?" I asked taking advantage of her light mood. I really, really wanted to give her a reason to laugh again.

"Okay, well, I have to tell it as a story," she began. "But aren't you here to see someone?"

I had completely forgotten about Wally! "Oh, yes! My friend. He got shot during a robbery, but he's okay now. Hopefully, I'll be taking him home today or tomorrow. I think they just want to make sure an infection doesn't set in. How about you?"

"I'm here with my mother. She had a heart attack a couple of days ago. She's a teacher at Bear Creek Elementary School. She's retiring soon, and I told her…anyway, she's doing better but she still has a few days to go before we can talk about going home."

"I hope she has a complete and speedy recovery," I said softly.

"Me too. Anyway, we're swapping family tree stories," she seemed totally delighted to be talking about something other than death and the threat of death. She'd had too much loss already.

"Okay, well, it all began many years ago. My great-great-great-grandmother was born into a large family. Back in those days, appearances were everything, even at the expense of a family member, if they were an embarrassment to the family unit."

"Not like today when we parade our crazy relatives around and sit them on the porch and serve them cocktails!" I laughed.

"So true!" she agreed.

"So, and this is where the skeletons start to pile up. My, I'll just say first grandmother, got pregnant and was banned from the family. Her older sister took her away to Pennsylvania to have the baby."

A wave of ice flowed through my veins. Could this be? No, not possible, but I had to hear the entire story.

"My first grandmother died in childbirth, so my, ummm...first aunt took the baby and cared for her. She assumed her sister's name, so the baby would never know her mother died giving birth to her."

"What...what..." I stuttered, "What was your first grandmother's name?"

"Same as mine, Rosa Hargate. Well, mine is Rosa Hargate Kendall."

Chapter Thirty-Three

I don't know if I passed out or what, but the next thing I knew, I was laying on the floor with a nurse waving something under my nose. I pushed her away.

Rosa looked horrified, the nurse looked worried, and I was humiliated. I wanted out of there as quickly as possible!

I struggled to sit up, refusing advice to 'take it slow'. I began to sweat, all at once, copious amounts. I couldn't get enough air into my lungs and my muscles felt like jelly.

Corinthia was looking on in interest saying, "That was so cool!"

The little knot of people standing over me began to lose interest once they realized I wasn't dying or anything.

"I have to go," I mumbled.

"You really should rest a minute," the nurse said for the umpteenth time. "They're bringing you some orange juice. Do you have sugar issues? Are you diabetic? What's the last thing you remember?"

I just wanted out. "No. No. And I don't remember." I sat up and hoisted myself into the nearest chair just trying to get my breath.

"Are you sure you're okay?" Rosa said taking my hand.

"Yeah, I'm great, I think I should have had breakfast this morning," I said trying to muster up a reassuring smile for her.

It all made sense now, even the elementary school fire. Rosa's mother was a teacher there. Brendore must not have been able to get any information from her, so he burned the school and then caused her to have a heart attack. He was eliminating the family one by one.

I turned to her and with all the courage I could give her, I said, "Rosa, I would love to hear more! I'm so embarrassed I picked this time to get stupid and pass out, but I do need to go see my friend. I really have to go now."

I stood on shaking legs and while I would like to say I practically ran out of the waiting room, I'm sure the security video showed someone with one too many of my mother's magic cookies in their system, trying to figure out where the hell the floor went.

I couldn't wait to tell Wally that we'd finally found our Rosa! Then, just as I was about to walk into his room, I knew I couldn't tell a soul about this. Hopefully, I hadn't put her and Corinthia in danger by speaking out loud about it.

I heard running footsteps behind me. Bracing myself for whatever Brendore was going to do to me next, I heard, "Skunk!"

I whirled around to see Corinthia staring up at me.

"You forgot your phone. I got it fixed for you," she said.

I bent down and hugged her, "Thank you, Corrie. Thank you!"

She wiggled out of my embrace and backed away from me, "You're really weird."

I composed myself and went in to see Wally. He was sitting up in bed, channel surfing and an older woman sat beside him knitting.

"Hey, Red!" he called out to me.

"Hey, yourself, big guy. How are you doing today?"

He wiggled a little in the narrow bed and grinned, "Like I got hit by a Mack Truck, but all things considered, I woke up on the green side of the grass, so I'm good. For someone who got shot."

The woman looked over her reading glasses but never missed a stitch.

"Oh, hey, this is my mom. Mom, this is Red. Red, this is my mom," he introduced us.

"You suck at introductions, Wallace," I scolded.

He only laughed at me. I reached out my hand in greeting. She hesitated, then took it and shook it with all the strength of a wet washcloth.

"You can call me Mrs. Jenkins," she said giving me the stink eye.

"Mom, be nice. We talked about this. None of this is Red's fault. Shit happens, I told you that," he said silently begging his mother to just play nice.

"I'm sorry. It's just that my son gets shot and I have to hear about it from him as he lays in his hospital bed! Seems like someone could have called me! You have any idea what it's like to get a phone call like that?"

I felt properly chastised. I was so used to taking care of myself, I didn't even take the time to call his parents. Of course, they were worried. I wasn't used to caring for anyone but myself. I hadn't even called my own parents when I was so badly injured. I could have been killed in those woods and they would have gotten the news on the nightly news program. I had fleetingly thought of calling Wally's parents and then just put it out of my mind. I suppose her chilly demeanor was warranted.

"I am so sorry, Mrs. Jenkins, you are so right! Please, accept my apologies," I acquiesced.

She softened up a bit, "Well, it's okay. At least, he's going to be good as new. I'm trying to tell him he needs to come home with me. We got a notice from the school that he'd dropped out, again, no courtesy phone call, and should have known…"

"I promise, next time, I'll call you first," I promised hoping this was the right thing to say. Apparently not.

"NEXT TIME? Young lady, are you trying to kill our son?" she yelled.

Feeling like a cornered wild animal, I glanced at Wally, who was thoroughly enjoying every minute of this. "I have to go! Call me if you need anything, or not. I don't know…Anyway, bye!"

My escape from the hospital was sweet, until I got to my car. I was experimenting with driving myself, and doing an okay job, even with my arm in a cast. Then, like a lightning bolt, it hit me. Wally had dropped out of school! That wasn't part of our agreement! I loved having him with me on these adventures, but they didn't pay the rent, so to speak. We would be having a little chat about this when he got home.

I unlocked the front door and entered my sanctuary. It was cool and even the bright sunshine seemed to be respectful of my stress level. I closed every blind, every curtain, locked the doors and windows. I lay on the bed. Spirit came over and laid his head on my tummy.

"How are we going to play this?" I asked him. He didn't talk much or often so I wasn't expecting him to answer. He looked at me with soulful eyes.

"We're so close!" I whined. "I just don't know what to do to keep everyone safe. If Rocco and Brendore find out I've found Rosa, then I'm pretty certain he will kill them. However,

I need to get the money to them without their knowledge. Give me some ideas!"

"Well, I do have one," Spirit said softly.

I bolted to sit on the edge of the bed. "I'm all ears, buddy."

I heard Miss Vera knock on the door and call out, "Yoo-hoo, Probably?"

Tap, tap. Tap. If I didn't answer, maybe she would go away. I had too many thoughts stampeding around in my head. It was giving me a headache.

But, after all, she was generous without getting much in return. I suppose social convention says I should be polite.

I went to the door and opened it to Miss Sunshine, herself.

"Hey, Miss Vera," I gave her a quick hug.

"I was making some Banana Nut Bread this morning and thought maybe you would like some. So good when it's hot and fresh, slathered with a sinful amount of butter!" she chattered as she walked to the kitchen. "My! It certainly is dark in here! Why don't we open...Oh dear, were you getting ready to take a nap?"

I put an arm around her and leaned over her shoulder sniffing the oven-fresh bread. "No, not really. I just got home from   the   hospital.

"Oh, how is that precious boy?" she asked with total sincerity. She and Aunt Jo were polar opposites.

"He's doing well. Hopefully coming home tomorrow," I said watching her slice the bread into thick slices. I went to the fridge and got butter and two dessert plates.

"Anything interesting happen at the hospital?" she asked matter-of-factly. That right there told me she knew very well something did. Coordinator! Had she orchestrated the meeting with Rosa? Sweet Miss Vera was full of quiet surprises.

"No, not really," I said equally mater-of-fact.

She smiled and nodded her head knowingly.

We chatted about the upcoming spring and how we hoped there wasn't so much rain this time around. When we finished our bread, she got up to leave.

"One must never take their guardian angels for granted," she said out of the blue, "Even the ones who don't seem so angelic."

I knew right away she was talking about Aunt Jo. My Aunt Jo was quirky, rude, blunt, and lacked social graces, and I loved her more than life itself. There was a certain comfort when she was around. Truth be told, she kind of sucked as a Protector, but she always managed to get things to turn out okay. Kind of like a drunk fairy godmother.

"It takes all kinds, Miss Vera," I said giving in to the urge to hug her again.

She giggled and then cleared her throat. She got to within inches of my face, "Be careful, Probably. Never let your guard down with Brendore. He may seem weak to you, but up to this point, he has only been toying with you. Hoping to scare you off."

My stomach clenched. She was right and I knew it, I just didn't want to admit it. I liked feeling like the victor, but in reality, I was only play-acting. I'd seen weird, supernatural things in the past year, but it wasn't even the tip of the iceberg.

"Miss Vera, there's something that's been bothering me about all this, since the beginning."

"What, dear?"

"Why does Brendore and Rocco want that money so bad? What could two dead guys do with that much money?" I asked.

Miss Vera shook her head, "I can't say for sure, but the chatter is that there is a certain senator that would benefit greatly from it. Unfortunately, it would cause much suffering for everyone else. They must NOT get that money under any circumstances!"

Spirit walked into the living room for a drink of water. Miss Vera lit up. "Rubio! You seem like you've healed nicely!"

"Spirit. That's Spirit, Miss Vera," I reminded her.

She looked a little confused and then smiled with her entire face, "Oh, my! I meant Spirit. Good heavens, where is my mind these days?"

With that, she stepped outside and returned to her house.

The house felt empty and dark without her. I went through and opened every blind, and even opened a window or two to let some fresh air in. I had a lot to do in a short period of time.

I went to the bookcase and took down *Guide to Telemarketing* and removed the letter. The clue was here. I just knew it was. I had inspected and analyzed this letter a million times. Well, that might be a bit of an exaggeration, but I had looked at it from every angle possible. No clues jumped out at me. I laid it on my desk and just stared at it chewing my lower lip in concentration.

I'm not aware of how much time passed, I just know I jerked my head up and realized I'd been laying in a puddle of drool. Gross, to say the least. I swiped at my mouth and cheek and went to fetch a paper towel to mop up the rest. I picked up the letter to blot it when I saw something that looked like words. I held it up to the window. I felt my heart rate increase. Those splotches of blood, the saliva was causing a chemical reaction of some kind. Each splatter contained a word!

Chapter Thirty-Four

Rosa/Peter
Marjorie Mae   *1865*
Corinthia Louise   *1882*
David Owen-D   *1902-1904*
LouEllan June   *1905*
Jennifer Marie   *1924*
Elizabeth Rosa   *1945*
Rosa Hargate   *1975*
Corinthia Nicole   *2005*

There was no doubt this was Rosa and Peter's family tree. Peter had died many years ago at the ripe old age of eighty-seven. Who had been keeping track of the births? Who had this letter before me? Could it have been Lydia Jackson before her death? You know, that kind of made sense now. She kept talking about me having something that belonged to her. She was the one tracking down the family! She had been obsessed with finding the money and the only way she could do that was that she happened upon the letter and decided to do her own ancestry research. Apparently, Brendore was aware of this, which was why he wasn't interested in the letter. He already knew what it contained, but it did not contain the location of the money! That's why he needed *me* to find it for him! The real Lydia Jackson was also looking for it, but she was going about it the only way she knew how.

I sat back, stunned. On the one hand, thank you, Lydia! On the other hand, how cold and calculating to hunt down a family's history of tragedy and life, for her own personal gain. She must have inadvertently, (giving her a benefit of doubt) accepted the help of Rocco and Brendore. Once she opened that Pandora's Box, there was no closing the lid. I just couldn't believe she was into the political scam, she wanted it for herself. I wondered if Brendore and Rocco arranged her departure from the world of the living for just that reason.

My eyes darted to the fireplace. No one knew that stuffed into the chimney were three duffel bags full of money. We started to count it and stopped at $1.2M. That sure would go a long way to helping Corinthia and her mother. Now, to get the money to them.

That night, I slept better than I'd slept in months and months. Life seemed organized once again. Answers had been found to nagging questions. Spirit and I formed battle plan. I would beat Brendore at his own game. I may not be able to defeat him in war, but I was pretty sure I would win this battle.

In the morning, on my way to the hospital, I made a couple of stops. I went in to see Wally. His mother was gone, and he was eating breakfast, or trying to. I watched him let the soupy oatmeal slide out of the spoon and plop thickly back into the bowl. I don't even think he realized the look of disgust on his face. He looked at me as I came through the doorway and brightened immediately.

"Hey, Red!" he said happily.

"Hey, yourself. I see they brought you a gourmet breakfast again."

He gave me that look that said, *hardy-har-har.*

"I really miss your cooking," he said pitifully, "And Miss Vera's! I think they're trying to kill me in here."

I laughed at his drama queen tantrum, "Well, you'll be coming home soon. What do you want for your first meal in freedom?"

"I want BBQ, coleslaw, fresh tomatoes, steak, fries, strawberry shortcake, green beans, ham, yeast rolls…"

I held up my hands in surrender, "Okay. Okay, I get it. Waffle House it is then!"

He laughed. "Seriously, though, Doc came by last night and said if I had a good night and I pooped this morning, I could go home."

"That's wonderful!" I said a little too enthusiastically, "I mean, Spirit really misses you."

"What about you? Have you missed me?" he asked slyly.

"*Pffft.* You mean having the house all to myself so I can come and go as I please? Eat what I want? Take naps when I want?"

He looked a little hurt, but then a smile played on his lips, "Yeah, I missed you too."

The doctor came in with a glance in my direction, but then he did a double-take. I could see the wheels turning, but I didn't care. He consulted his charts.

"How are you feeling this morning?"

"Good."

"Any new pains anywhere?"

"Nope."

"Have you had a morning BM?"

"Doc, you would have been proud!"

The doctor gave a crooked smile.

"Well, then I hereby release you!"

With a snap of the chart, the rustle of paper being removed, and a click of his pen, the doctor left the room.

"You lied," I pointed out.

My only answer was a guilty grin.

He was eventually processed and loaded into the wheelchair for the ride to the car. The nurse was listing do's and don'ts and greeting other personnel. Wally wasn't paying attention at all; he was just happy to be going home.

Once we were settled in the car, I turned to him, "Your mother doesn't like me."

He laughed, "Oh, she's okay once you get to know her. She really didn't mean anything by it. She just doesn't know what to think of you."

"Well, why didn't you tell me you dropped out of school? I thought part of our agreement was that you would finish school?" I pressed on. Lots of people didn't know what to think of me. This was old news.

"I meant to. It's just everything started happening and the time never seemed like the right time. I'm sorry. If it's any consolation, I didn't tell anyone," he said in his defense.

"Okay, whatever. Seriously, though, you want to stop for something to eat?" I suggested after deciding this conversation was boring.

"Sure," he agreed. "By the way, anything new on Spook News?"

"I can't talk about it, but I need your help," I said vaguely.

"Okay, but don't I need to know in order to help you?" he asked.

"You're on a need to know status and right now you don't need to know."

He wasn't satisfied, but he dropped it. He knows me so well.

I was anxious for the evening. I laid out several piles of paper on the table. I had a stack of twenty's and a few hundreds as well. Wally's eyes got big. "What's all this?"

"Shut up and sit down and start cutting this stack of papers the same size as the money," I pointed to a chair.

He did. Nice thing about Wally, he never questioned me. We made short work of it and soon had stacks of fake money all over the kitchen table. I retrieved three cheaply made duffle bags I had purchased at the dollar store and began to just stuff the 'money' in them. Wally followed suit.

When we finished, he looked at our handiwork, "I'm not going to pretend I know what this is all about, but now what?"

"We wait," I said.

As the evening began to move in and the light became a soft purple, I went out to the backyard and started a fire.

"I need you to follow my lead," I whispered. He nodded.

As the flames began to grow, I opened a duffle bag and withdrew a stack of money and threw it on the fire. Sparks danced toward the night sky.

"I cannot wait to get rid of this damned money!" I said loudly. "It's done nothing but cause trouble!"

"Almost got me killed!" Wally chimed in throwing another stack in the flames.

"If it's gone, then no one gets anything," I added. "Throw it on there like you mean it!"

I was beginning to think my plan wasn't going to work. We were getting down to the last few stacks. From the corner of my eye, I saw a shadow. I drew in a deep breath and hoped we were ready for this.

"What are you doing?" came the familiar voice and Lydia Jackson stepped out of the shadows.

"I'm sick of this!" I cried. "I'm burning the money! It's cursed! I hate it!"

Lydia's eyes bugged out. "NO!" she screamed as she tried to snatch a bundle from me. I twisted it from her grasp and threw it into the growing flames.

Wally pulled another bundle out of the bags. "We're almost done, Red! Gone forever!"

Lydia ran to him and tried to save the money. He held it high in the air, "You want this?"

Lydia began to seethe. The bags still gave the appearance they were still full, so she ran for them. I snatched them up and tossed one to Wally. I threw duffle bag and all onto the fire.

Lydia morphed into Brendore, then Lydia, then Brendore. The shape grew, elongated, an ear-splitting shriek emanated from the creature. It darted toward the flames. Wally threw his duffle bag into the flames. The demon screamed and roared. It tried to go into the flames, but it screamed in frustration.

I began to laugh hysterically. "You thought you would win, Brendore! You want the money? Go get it!"

I threw my last bundle in the fire. Sparks showered and began a circular motion. It looked like a tornado filled with fire. Brendore screamed. Black, diaphanous arms grabbed at the floating ashes, the whirlwind of smoke and fire going faster and faster. Wally and I took a few steps back mesmerized at the violence of the dervish.

"You will die! I will kill you myself!" screamed Brendore/Lydia. "You will die!"

Suddenly, it was quiet. Wally and I looked at each other, wondering what was coming next.

The fire crackled, the burned paper curled. The duffle bags sent up gray smoke as they smoldered, then caught fire for the final destruction. A breeze softly brought the promise of spring.

"I guess that's it," I said, unsure of what to do next. It was hard to believe it was finally over.

"I'm hungry," Wally announced, "And for once, I didn't get maimed, beaten, or shot!"

I shook my head at him and went into the house.

Chapter Thirty-Five

"**W**hat do you want for breakfast?" Rosa asked a sleepy Corrie.

"Can I have a Twinkie?" she asked.

"No, you can't have a Twinkie, but I can make you some chocolate chip pancakes. Would that be just as good?" Rosa said with a smile.

Corrie rubbed the sleep from her eyes and nodded, trying to hide her smile.

The doorbell rang, "Hold on to those happy thoughts, I'll be right back."

Rosa went to the door and opened it. No one stood on the porch. She looked both ways and down the street. She was just about to close the door when she noticed three duffle bags leaning against the house.

Confused she bent down and looked at them closely. She checked once again to see if anyone was nearby. She unzipped one and saw the corner of money. Her heart skipped a beat. She took all three into the house and sat them on the coffee table. She hesitated not sure how to proceed. A bank robbery? Why would the thieves leave the money on her doorstep?

She opened each bag and counted the money. It smelled kind of musty. At the bottom of one of the bags, she found an envelope. She picked it up and examined it. It was a very old letter. She opened it and read the love letter. She felt tears puddle in her eyes. Another slip of paper was in the envelope.

"Dear Rosa,

This money belongs to you. It took a journey of two hundred years to get to you. I hope you will use it to give you and Corrie a better life. Your great-great-great-great grandfather and grandmother, Peter Euclid and Rosa Hargate, want you to have it.

I'm so sorry you can't use it to bring Brian back, but I know he would want to know you and his daughter are well taken care of.

Be well, be happy, and don't ever pass the chance for love.

Wally and I watched while peeking through the window from the outside. I looked behind Rosa and saw Peter and Rosa with arms around each other, smiling at their granddaughter. Peter looked at me, smiled, and nodded.

I gave him a smile and a thumbs up. We slid down the side of the house and giggled. I couldn't resist one last peek. Wally pulled me back down and gave me a celebratory kiss without the tongue action.

I hope you enjoyed the first Probably Magic adventure! Stay tuned for the second book: *Probably Magic and The Wheel of Misfortune*

Oh, what has she gotten herself into now?

If you enjoyed this story, please be so kind as to leave a review on Amazon.com and any of your favorite book nooks. Reviews are the lifeblood for authors.

I invite you to also check out the first series, The Old Man and The Watch.

Book One: The Old Man and The Watch: Searching For the Long Road HOME

Book Two: The Good Guardian: The Battle of Grey Island

Book Three: SnakeSkin: Alone in the Time Zone

Book Four: The Glory Plains: The Raising of a Thousand Voices

Book Five: Tale of Oak: Coming HOME

Author Jo Jewell

I call myself a mountain woman. In truth, I was born on the flatlands of Indiana on May 20th, 1955. The world population was 2.780 billion, Eisenhower was President, unemployment was 5.5%, Cher was nine years old on that day, and you could mail a letter for .03 cents. Luckily, the dinosaurs were gone, and fire had been invented by then. I moved to Tennessee to the foot of The Great Smoky Mountains in 1998.

I have been writing since the age of six. I won my first regional poetry contest in second grade. For the past 50+ years, I have written for myself and only a chosen few. Writing to me is as life-sustaining as breathing, as important as a beating heart. I have written for newspapers, had my own local column in the Blount County Voice, shared stories of my life for my friends to make them laugh, sigh, cry, or more importantly, to think. I wrote puppet shows for our mentally handicapped facility, inspirational short stories for church services, and a series of articles that led to testimony before the Maryland State Senate and the creation of the bill: Maryland Task Force for Abused, Abandoned, and Neglected Children. As long as it meant I could write, I wrote. I can't tell you where this passion came from, I can't tell you one incident that caused me to start writing and not stop. I have no memory of "starting" to write, I just did, and at a very early age.

I hope you enjoy reading this story as much as the characters enjoyed telling their stories.